Twice the Lie

A DI Erica Swift Thriller

M K Farrar

Published by Warwick House Press, 2021.

This is a work of fiction. Similarities to real people, places, or events are entirely coincidental.

TWICE THE LIE

First edition. March 10, 2021.

Copyright © 2021 M K Farrar.

Written by M K Farrar.

Chapter One

"Come on, Liam," Conner Lowry called over his shoulder as he traipsed across the fields towards the small copse of trees ahead.

Liam Gilbert slowed his pace and wrapped his arms around his body. He'd been hot from all the walking and had taken off his jacket and tied it around his waist, but there was a chill in the air, and his trainers were wet from the damp grass.

"Nah." He shook his head. "I need to get back soon or my mum's going to have a fit."

Conner put out his lower lip in a mock pout. "Aww, is Mummy going to smack your botty. Poor baby."

Liam wasn't a baby. He was eleven years old and would be going to high school—or secondary school as his mum kept calling it—in September. Conner was going to a different school, and though Liam never would have said it out loud, he was kind of relieved about that. Conner was only four months older, but he acted like it was four years, always harping on about how he was the eldest, like it made him more mature when the opposite was true. Liam liked Conner, but sometimes he could be a bit of a bully, and, as his mum kept telling him, the only way to deal with bullies was by standing up to them.

He took a few extra steps to catch up with Conner and punched him in the arm. "Don't call me a baby."

"Get lost, dickhead," Conner exclaimed. "No one gets away with hitting me."

He took the punch as an invitation to fight and jumped on Liam, hooking his arm around Liam's neck, grinding his knuckles into the top of his head.

"Hey, get the hell off me," Liam protested, shoving Conner away.

His friend only laughed, taking the whole thing as one big game. It wasn't a game. The top of Liam's head hurt now.

Conner never seemed to care what anyone thought, and his way of always pushing things a little too far was typical of him. Liam wished he was braver and could stand up to him a bit more, but he knew what Conner's reaction would be. He'd laugh and call Liam a pussy and make chicken noises. Then he'd go into school and tell everyone that Liam was all those things and more.

"Come on, it's not far now." Conner was already striding on ahead. "We'll walk through the woods, then we'll be back on the road. The shop's not far from there. I've got a couple of quid. I'll treat you to something."

Liam perked up at the promise of food. Maybe Conner could be all right. Mum wouldn't be happy if she found out he'd been snacking right before dinner, but as long as he got rid of the rubbish before getting home and made sure his face and clothes were free of crumbs, she would never know.

They reached the line of trees and ducked between the branches. The canopy blocked out the late-afternoon sunlight. Liam shivered and quickly tensed his muscles and cast a furtive glance towards Conner, hoping his friend hadn't noticed. It would be something else for Conner to pick on him about, pointing and laughing that Liam was scared.

The road wasn't far away, just past a few more trees. Liam pushed on, overtaking Conner, wanting to be out of the claustrophobic feel of the branches stretching over him. He imagined them moving, swiping down to hit him across the back of the head, or for roots to burst from the ground and wrap around his ankles.

He stepped out into a small clearing and exhaled a breath. He could see the sky again—darkening, but still blue—and, through the trees on the other side of the clearing, the road was visible. Too visible. A line of crushed bushes and wrecked saplings created a tunnel through the rest of the trees.

Conner came to a halt beside him. "Holy shitballs!"

But his friend wasn't looking at the road or the tunnel through the trees and bushes. Instead, his head was turned in the opposite direction, over his shoulder to their left.

Liam followed his line of sight.

He gasped and staggered back. "Oh, shit."

A car was at a standstill, the bonnet crumpled like an accordion against a tree trunk. The tree leaned heavily to one side, as though the force of the impact had dislodged its firm rooting into the ground and left it at an angle.

Liam pulled himself together. "How long do you think it's been here?"

Conner shook his head. "Dunno. Not long."

Steam or smoke rose from the bonnet in a ribbon of white.

Conner's blue eyes brightened with excitement. "There might be someone in there."

Someone who was hurt. Or even worse.

Liam took a step back. "We should go get help."

Conner laughed. "Don't be a dumbass. I've got my phone. We can call the police."

Despite the circumstances, Liam's cheeks heated with shame. It was just another thing that made Conner always seem and act cooler and better than him. Liam didn't have his own phone. His mum said he could have one once he started his new school, but that hadn't happened yet. Conner only had a phone 'cause his parents had separated, and his dad had bought him one so they could stay in touch, but that wasn't the point.

"Oh, yeah, right. Do that then."

Conner had taken his phone out of his pocket, but his gaze remained glued on the smoking car. "Do you think it might blow up?"

"I don't know, Conner. Just call the police, will you."

Still, Conner made no move to do so. "Let's take a quick look inside first. How can we tell the police what we've found if we don't even know ourselves yet?"

Someone might be bleeding to death in the driver's seat. They didn't have time to be messing around. But a combination of fear and self-consciousness held Liam's tongue, and no argument left his lips.

Conner was close to the car now—only a couple of feet away. If the vehicle *did* explode, it would take Conner down with it. It would also take Conner's phone, which would leave Liam out here alone, with no way of contacting anyone, and pieces of his friend's body all over the place.

"Conner, be careful!" he said.

"Pussy," Conner threw back at him and took another step closer. "Oh, fuck. There's blood!"

Liam swallowed hard and turned his face away. What if there was a body? He grew dizzy at the prospect, his mouth flooding with spit. No, he couldn't throw up. That wouldn't be a good idea at all. Conner would never let him live it down. He fought against the urge, breathing through his need to puke and willing away the rush of heat that affected his face. The seconds ticked by, threatening to become minutes, and finally he managed to get a hold on himself.

When he turned back, Conner was right beside the car, his face pressed to the passenger side window.

"There's loads of blood. You have to see this, Liam!"

Despite his nerves, Liam was still just a boy, and the promise of seeing something gruesome lured him in. He took the few steps needed to bring him in line with Conner and peered into the car.

Red was splattered like paint across the cracked glass spiderweb glass of the windscreen and the dark-grey plastic of the dashboard. For a moment, he thought someone was hunched over the steering wheel, but then it dawned on him that it was the partially deflated airbag. The windscreen was crumpled, and more blood covered the airbag.

Liam frowned and glanced at Conner. Instead of finding the driver, folded over the steering wheel or slumped against the driver's door, the seat was empty.

The driver wasn't there.

Chapter Two

"Call for you, boss."

DI Ryan Chase yanked his thoughts away from his latest case file to see the landline phone on his desk flashing.

"Thanks, Swift," he said, nodding to his detective sergeant who'd answered the call at her desk on the other side of the office.

He picked up the handset. "DI Chase."

"This is Police Sergeant Fortum, from the Avon and Somerset Police," a female voice said. "I've got a situation you may find of interest. A car accident."

"You've called the wrong team then. You need to contact the Roads Policing Unit."

Ryan was part of the Major Crimes Investigation Team in Bristol. Over the past fifteen years, since he'd moved from his hometown of Plymouth in his late twenties, he had worked his way from a detective constable to sergeant and was now a detective inspector.

"I've contacted them as well," she continued, "but they suggested your team might need to get involved since it appears as though there's been the possibility of foul play."

He straightened in his seat. "You've got a body?"

"Not exactly. We have a missing body."

"A missing body? There's no murder if there's no body."

"If there hasn't been a murder, someone's done a *Carrie* job on the inside of the vehicle that two boys, both aged eleven, found."

His interest had been piqued. "What's the location?"

Fortum told him an area north-east of Bristol city, off the A420, where the housing estates gave way to fields and woodland.

"Okay. I'll be there in twenty minutes, depending on traffic." He glanced at his watch. They'd hit the tail end of rush hour. Traffic in the city was bad enough during most times of the day, but by six p.m. it was gridlocked. "Actually, make that thirty."

He hung up. "Swift, we're needed on a case. You up for it?"

She was already on her feet, plucking her grey suit jacket from the back of her chair. "Are you kidding? Anything to get out of the office."

The New Bridewell Police Station was a tall glass-and-concrete structure located in the middle of Bristol city centre. A white, blue, and yellow squad car sat parked out the front on the other side of the silver security bollards that protected the entrance.

Ryan glanced at the plaque on the wall.

Serve, Protect, Respect.

He did his best.

"We'll take my pool car." He snatched his keys from his desk and followed her out.

A NARROW COUNTRY LANE that could barely fit two vehicles driving in opposite directions wound between the tall hedgerows. Beyond the hedges were fields and the spattering of woodland where the car had been found by two local boys.

They'd passed a couple of cottages, a tiny newsagent, and a run-down pub advertising OAP two-for-one meals on a Tuesday farther down the lane, but that was it as far as civilisation went. There were several other villages that had gradually blended into the outskirts of Bristol over the years, but they were a couple of miles away.

"What were the boys doing all the way out here?" Swift said. "How old did you say they were?"

"They're both eleven." Ryan kept his eyes on the road as he drove. "Final year of primary school, I think that makes them."

"Sounds about right, though I can't say I've paid too much attention to school years. We're a little way off that yet with Poppy," she said, mentioning her baby daughter.

"You'd think we'd remember better since we were both children ourselves."

"That was more recent for one of us than the other," she said with a grin.

Erica Swift had been working for him for the past twelve months, and, though she was barely thirty, she had already proven herself as a competent, reliable detective. She had a young family, but she'd managed to successfully juggle the demands of the job and having a baby, though much of that was down to the help of her husband at home.

Ryan was in the same position, except it was his wife who took care of things at home. He also had a daughter—a slightly older girl, Hayley, who, at five, was as sassy as they came. He always told people she was five going on fifteen, but the truth was that he had no idea how to actually handle having a teenage daughter, and he wasn't relishing the prospect either. Still, that was a long way off. Ten years and he'd be approaching fifty with a teenager. It seemed almost impossible to believe.

Hayley had started school recently, so Chase had paid a *little* more interest in how the school years worked, or as little as he'd thought he could get away with. It was one of the things his wife, Donna, liked to complain about. She always said the only thing that really interested him in life was his work. When they'd first met, he'd thought she'd liked that about him—his intensity and dedication—but as the years had passed, the things she'd found most interesting about him in the early days had become the same things that had driven them apart. Not that they were officially separated, but he could sense it looming on the horizon like the threat of a storm. They were careful around each other now, choosing their words with the same caution a landmine-clearing expert might use to pick his next step. They both knew they were one big argument away from one of them—most likely him—finding somewhere else to live, and while neither of them really wanted that to happen, it almost felt out of their hands. Their fate, it seemed, had already been decided, but they were just trying to put off the inevitable for as long as they could.

A marked police car blocked the road. Ryan slowed and lowered his window, showing the attending officer his ID and getting nodded through. He pulled the car up behind a police van and switched off the engine. There was no pavement, and he and Swift climbed out of the car onto the road.

Even without the uniformed officers guarding the way, it would have been easy to spot the location of the crash. The car had ploughed a tunnel through the hedgerow and saplings, to come to a halt against a bigger tree. The silver paintwork was just visible through all the foliage.

"This way," he said to Erica, taking the lead.

People in white protective outerwear worked inside an inner cordon. They mainly focused on the car but were also setting markers down beside items outside of the vehicle they clearly thought might be important.

An attractive woman around his age—mid-forties—with her dead-straight dark hair cut into a severe bob with a fringe, turned to meet them. It was the police sergeant who was co-ordinating the scene, and the same one who'd called them in, Lauren Fortum.

"DI Chase," she greeted him. "Thanks for coming."

"Of course. You remember my sergeant, DS Swift."

The two women shook hands.

"Good to have you along," Fortum said.

Ryan glanced over at the scene. "What have we got?"

"Right now, not much, except a missing driver and a blood bath inside the car. The registered keeper of the vehicle is a Mrs Elizabeth Lloyd of two-three-six Gilham Road, Bristol, but of course that doesn't mean it was her who was driving."

"Has the car been reported stolen?" he asked.

"Not yet. I've got officers going around to the address to find out. It might just be that the owners haven't noticed it's gone. Looks like the vehicle swerved off the road and crashed through a number of bushes until it slammed into the tree."

"It must have still been doing some speed to cause that kind of damage," Erica said.

Fortum nodded. "Yes, it seems that way."

"Any skid marks on the road?" Ryan asked. "Signs the brakes were used?"

"Not that we've found, but we have a Forensic Collison Investigator working on that."

"The brakes might not have been working," Erica suggested. "Or they didn't have time to use them."

"It's possible," Fortum said, "but the reason I've brought you here is less to do with the reason the car crashed and more to do with what happened to the driver afterwards."

Erica tipped her head to one side. "The two things might well be linked."

Ryan agreed. "I assume a search has already been done of the surrounding area and no one was found? Whoever was driving didn't manage to climb out of the car and then crawl into the woods?"

"My officers have done an initial search of the area, in case the driver was in a daze and wandered off and collapsed nearby, but we haven't found anything yet. There was a blood trail heading out towards the road, but then it stopped. I've requested the helicopter and a dog unit, but as you can see, they're not here yet."

"The doors were shut." Erica nodded to the car.

PS Fortum offered her a tight smile. "That's right. When the boys found the car, all the doors were already shut, so whoever was driving not only sustained the kind of injury to create that much blood, but also managed to climb out of the car and then bothered to shut the door behind them again. There was also significant damage to the steering column, but the key was missing from the ignition."

"There's the possibility more than one person was in the car," Ryan said. "If they weren't hurt so badly, they might have helped the driver out, took out the key, and then shut the car door."

"And not called an ambulance?" Erica frowned, her lips twisted. "The only reason they'd do that is if they didn't want to be caught driving the car."

Fortum raised her eyebrows. "Or didn't want to be caught at all."

Erica turned in the direction of the road. "If they got back to the road, someone might have picked them up."

"Considering the amount of blood inside the vehicle," Fortum said, "the driver would have been in a hell of a state. I find it hard to imagine someone would have picked them up without insisting on taking them to hospital, and I've had one of my officers call around, and no one matching the description of possible injuries has been brought in."

Ryan tightened his lips. "Unless it was someone they already knew. Someone who knew taking them to hospital would cause problems."

All of this was just speculation, of course. Until they had a report back from SOCO, they wouldn't know for sure how many people had been in the vehicle. There was blood spatter on both seats, but that could have happened after the accident and while they were trying to get out. Until forensics ran it, they wouldn't know if all the blood belonged to the same person.

Ryan considered the weather being a factor, but there wasn't any wind that might have blown the door shut, and the car was well sheltered in its current position. "Maybe one of the boys shut the door."

Fortum shook her head. "They said they didn't. They said they cupped their hands to the glass to look inside and when they saw all the blood, they called triple-nine."

"How did they call triple-nine?" Erica asked.

"The older one had a mobile phone."

Ryan rolled his eyes. "They'll be getting mobile phones at birth at this rate."

Fortum shrugged. "Well, in this case it was handy that he had it on him. They waited right here until the responding officers showed up. Their parents have been informed and are on their way."

"I'll want to talk to the boys, too," Ryan said.

"Of course. They've been separated and placed into the backs of two of the squad cars. I have my officers watching over them."

"Good. Any other witnesses?"

"Not so far. But we'll put out a social media request to see if anyone saw the accident or perhaps the car right before the accident."

Ryan furrowed his brow. "Surely someone would have called it in if they'd seen anything."

"Maybe, but you never know."

"I assume we're going to be all out of luck as far as CCTV goes all the way out here as well."

Fortum gave him an apologetic smile. "Nothing on the road, and definitely nothing here."

"There's a pub farther down the road," Erica said, "and the villages we came through have a couple of speed cameras as well. One of the houses might have CCTV cameras, or the pub. We should check the speed camera footage as it might have caught something."

The rumble of car engines approached and then cut off again.

A female voice called out, "Sarge, the boys' mothers are here."

Fortum threw Ryan a smile. "Best you go and hear their side of the story for yourselves."

Chapter Three

Erica Swift followed her boss back out to the road where two civilian vehicles had been blocked by the marked police car. Two women had been stopped by the uniformed officer, but they both had the same stance of craned necks and worried expressions as they tried to see past him.

"I want to talk to the boys before we let their mothers anywhere near them," Ryan said. "You take one, and I'll speak to the other. Make sure they don't give us any reason to suspect them of foul play. If their stories match up, we can let them go with their parents for the night and speak to them again tomorrow."

"Yes, boss."

They separated. Erica went to one of the police vehicles while Ryan took the other.

She reached the car and showed her ID to the uniformed officer standing nearby. He nodded at her and opened the back door. Right away, the boy inside swung his legs out of the car as though he thought he was going to get out, but Erica put out her hand to stop him, so he ended up sitting on the back seat with his feet on the road.

"Hi," she said, and dropped to a crouch to bring them both to a more equal level. "I'm DS Swift. What's your name?"

The boy eyed her mistrustfully. "Conner Lowry."

"How old are you Conner?"

"Eleven."

"The same age as your friend? Liam, isn't it?"

"Yeah, but I'm older."

He had a sulky way about him, as though her mere presence was an irritation. He didn't seem to want to meet her eye, but she had the feeling he would have been like that with any adult, and it wasn't just that she was a detective and he'd been a witness to a crime.

"The two of you are at school together?" she asked.

His gaze flicked to hers and shifted away again. "That's right."

"Can you tell me what you were doing before you found the car?"

She had to remind herself that he was just a child, though the length of his legs hinted at him being as tall as she was. She made sure she kept a light tone to her voice, imagining she was talking to her daughter, rather than this sullen boy.

He shrugged. "We were just hanging out. Walking and stuff."

"Do you often take this route? It's quite a long way from home, isn't it?"

"Sometimes. Liam wanted to turn back and go home, but I told him I'd buy some sweets at the shop if he kept going, so he did."

"What time do you think you saw the car?"

He blinked rapidly and twisted his hands in his lap "Not sure. Sometime after five. Maybe five thirty. Dunno. I wasn't really paying attention to the time."

Erica raised an eyebrow. "Even though your parents would have wanted you home?"

"Yeah, I s'pose. Didn't really think about it."

Typical of kids his age. Some of them didn't seem to have the part of their brain developed yet that allowed them to consider how others—namely their parents—would feel when they were late.

"So, you came across the car," Erica continued. "Which of you saw it first?"

"I did, I think."

She shifted her weight from one side to the other. "And then what did you do?"

"I went over and checked through the window."

"Which window?"

"The passenger side 'cause that's what we were closest to. I thought I was going to see the driver lying there, and figured he might need help or something, but there was no one there."

"Then what did you do?"

"I had my phone with me, so I called nine-nine-nine."

"You did a really good job by doing that," she said, and the boy sat up straighter, his chest puffing out.

"What about other people. Did you hear or see anyone else hanging around?"

He shook his head. "No, it was just us."

"And there was no sign of the driver?"

"No."

Her thighs were starting to ache from being crouched for so long. "Okay, thank you for your help, Conner. It looks like your mum is here to collect you, but we're probably going to need to speak to you again tomorrow. We'll let you get some rest first. I know you've had a big day."

He nodded but didn't say anything else. Erica stood and glanced over to where it looked as though DI Chase was done with the other boy. She walked back to join him, and they compared notes.

"Okay," Ryan said with a nod, "it looks as though they're both telling the same story.

The two mothers were both waiting anxiously, clearly worried about their children.

"It's okay, let them through," Ryan called out.

The uniformed officer stepped out of the way, and the two women hurried past.

"We got a call," the one with blonde hair said as they approached. "Our boys found a crashed car."

"That's right, but don't worry," he assured them. "They're both safe."

"Oh, thank God." The brunette clutched her hand to her chest. "Can we see them?"

"Sorry, what was your name?" Erica asked, needing to make sure they had the right people.

"I'm Philippa Lowry," the blonde said, "and this is Marie Gilbert."

"Liam's mum," Marie Gilbert added.

Erica nodded. "Of course. Come this way."

The boys' long legs and lanky torsos emerged from each of the vehicles.

Philippa Lowry rushed up to her son. "Oh my God, are you all right?"

The slightly taller of the two boys, with dark-blond hair and blue eyes, shrugged his mother away. "Yeah, Mum. I'm fine. Jeez, don't make a fuss."

The second boy allowed his mother to hug him, but his gaze shifted to his friend, as though checking he hadn't been seen.

"Thank you for coming," Erica said. "I'm DS Swift. We'll need to speak to both of the boys again in more detail. It's probably best we do it down at the station tomorrow since it's already getting late."

The lack of daylight wasn't going to help them when it came to the Scenes of Crime Officers checking over the car and surrounding area, or in them finding the missing driver. They'd bring in floodlights, but nothing beat regular daylight.

"Yes, of course," Philippa Lowry said, her face taut with worry. "Whatever we can do to help. I hope no one was hurt."

Her son glanced over at her—he was as tall as she was. "Mum, there's blood everywhere. Someone was definitely hurt."

Erica didn't miss the hint of pleasure and excitement in the boy's tone. "Unfortunately, it does look that way, which is why it's really important that you make sure you tell us everything you know, no matter how small or unimportant it might seem to you. Even the tiniest detail might help us."

It wasn't that she thought they had anything to do with the car or the missing driver, but there was always the chance an inquisitive boy might have done something to alter the crime scene before they'd arrived.

"So, we're okay to take them home?" Marie Gilbert asked.

Erica handed both the women her card. "Yes, but we'll need to question the boys soon, so expect a call."

Ryan stepped in, clearing his throat. "Actually, if I can just ask one more question before you go."

Both boys nodded obediently. The two women took notice of DI Chase, suddenly standing straighter and touching their hair. The blonde mother threw him an appreciative glance. It was something Erica had seen on many occasions. The combination of a suit, dark hair, and blue eyes that creased at the corners when he smiled—not that he smiled often—caught a little attention from the women he encountered.

"Are you sure you didn't do anything to the car after you found it?" he asked the boys. "You didn't open or close any doors for example?"

Conner Lowry shook his head. "We didn't touch the doors. We just looked through the window, I swear."

Their prints would be found on the door handle, if they did, assuming they didn't think to wipe them down.

Ryan nodded. "Okay, well, we'll speak to you again in more detail very soon."

With arms around their sons' shoulders, the two women thanked the detectives and hurried away with the boys.

"DI Chase," Sergeant Fortum called from the direction of the crime scene. "I've just had a call from one of the officers I sent to the registered keeper's house. You're going to want to get down there."

Ryan frowned. "What's happened?"

"They found two bodies at the address. A woman and a child. There hasn't been an official identification made yet, but we believe them to be Elizabeth Lloyd and her six-year-old daughter, Kiera Lloyd."

Erica's stomach twisted. She always struggled with cases that involved children. "Jesus."

"No sign of the husband?" Ryan asked.

Erica glanced at him. "You think he might have been driving the car?"

He shrugged. "It's certainly possible. He could have been making a getaway." Ryan addressed Fortum. "Do we have a name for the husband."

"Yes," she said. "Douglas Paul Lloyd, forty-two years old, same address."

"Let's get a PCN check on that name. Find out if he's already known to us."

Erica couldn't help wondering if the amount of blood found in the car was because the husband had been hurt in the attack. Had he been hurt by the wife and child, perhaps defending themselves? Or had he been hurt by whoever killed the wife and child, and he took the car and ran?

There was a third possibility.

"The husband might have been forced to drive," Erica said. "If there was someone in the passenger seat, it might have been the attacker making him drive and he swung the car off the road, perhaps hoping to injure the attacker and then escape."

Ryan's lips thinned. "Shit, we need CCTV footage. We need to know how many people were in the car when it crashed."

She followed her boss's train of thought with relative ease and picked up where he'd left off. "If it was only the husband driving, he was most likely responsible for killing his family, but if there was someone else in the car, then the husband was also a victim."

"Potentially."

"Or else he had a cohort, but either way, we don't know where he is. Has he been abducted or is he in hiding?"

Ryan grimaced. "I want to see that house so we can get a better idea of what happened in the time leading up to the crash."

As they headed back to the car, the Police Dog Unit showed up. If anyone was going to track down the missing driver, it would be them.

Overhead came the familiar thwack of helicopter blades approaching.

Douglas Lloyd, wherever he was, wouldn't get far.

Chapter Four

The tension in the car was palpable as they left the outskirts of Bristol and drove across the city to the address of the registered keeper, Elizabeth Lloyd. The worst of the rush-hour traffic that they'd encountered on the way to the scene of the car accident had dispersed, so they made good time.

When he'd got up that morning, Ryan hadn't been expecting to deal with not one, but two new interlinked crimes. That was one thing he enjoyed about the job—no two days were ever the same. He doubted he'd be the only detective at the scene—a double murder was a big deal—but he wanted to see the second crime scene for himself so he could try to get an idea about how it had evolved from the crashed car and the missing driver.

Not that he took any pleasure in there having been a double murder, and attending the scene of a death of a child was always harder than that of an adult.

Beside him, in the passenger seat, Swift was quiet, too, her face angled away from him to look out of the passenger window as he drove. Her strawberry-blonde hair was pulled back from her face and tied in a no-nonsense bun at her nape. She wore little makeup, not that makeup was something she even needed.

The Scenes of Crime van had arrived quickly—Ryan assumed they were already inside the house, photographing and tagging any evidence—and uniformed officers were working to keep people away from the house. Squad cars blocked the road at either end, preventing anyone from driving through. Even people who lived here would be made to park their cars on a different street, and an officer would walk them home.

Just as he'd done at the scene of the crash, Ryan slowed the car and put down his window to show his ID to the officer running the blockade. The officer nodded his greeting, though his expression was grim, and waved the car through.

The house had been cordoned off, as had the part of the street directly in front of the property.

Ryan parked the car and climbed out, Swift getting out of the passenger side. He checked for who was co-ordinating the scene.

A different police sergeant was already on the scene—an older man Ryan had worked with several times before. Charles Pixello.

His thin lips pressed so tightly together, they almost vanished. Pixello was nearly bald, just a few strands sticking up comically from an otherwise bare head. Ryan didn't know why he didn't just have done with it and shave them off, but perhaps Pixello simply didn't care.

"DI Chase," Pixello said, greeting them. "Fucking awful business. I hear you were already on scene where the car was found when we discovered the bodies."

"That's right. No sign of the driver, though, or if there were any passengers."

"You think it was the husband who was driving?"

"Until we get forensics from inside the car, it's impossible to tell, though if it wasn't him, we haven't been able to locate him to notify him." He nodded towards the house. "Tell me about this one."

"Two bodies, mother and daughter, we believe. Thirty-five-year-old Elizabeth Lloyd and six-year-old Keira Lloyd. The mother had been stabbed, but as of yet, there's no sign of the murder weapon, and it would appear the girl was smothered or possibly strangled, but obviously we'll know more after a post-mortem."

"Any witnesses," Ryan asked, looking around.

The neighbours stood in the street or at their open front doors, their hands pressed to their mouths or shaking their heads at each other, ruminating about how awful it was that this terrible thing had happened and how they would never expect it in their quiet little street. From his experience, there was always someone in a street like this who knew everyone else's business and who probably couldn't wait to talk to the police.

"I've got my officers working their way through the neighbours, but not that we've found yet. I'm sure one of that lot will have seen something," Pixello said.

Ryan nodded his agreement. "Let's take a look inside."

They each pulled on protective outerwear before entering the property. The front door opened onto a small hallway, and directly ahead was the staircase. The first of the bodies lay sprawled across the bottom steps, the tiny feet still on the floor, her head pointed upwards.

The crumpled body of the small girl twisted him up inside. He'd been in the police for almost twenty years now and believed himself to be hardened to almost everything, but a dead child was hard not to feel emotional about. Could someone she'd loved have done this to her? He pictured her trusting that person, and the confusion and pain she would have felt in her final moments, and found himself bunching his fists, his jaw clenching. There should be a special place in hell for people who hurt children—not that Ryan really believed in such things.

Who had been killed first—the mother or daughter? Either way, the agony of one of them seeing the other murdered only served to increase his fury. Whether the mother had seen her daughter murdered, or the daughter had seen her mother killed, the pain would have been unbearable. No matter what he felt, he strived to remain professional, though he knew the emotion he was experiencing now would come out at some point, even if it was days or weeks later.

He nodded at the Scenes of Crime Officer as the other man moved around the property, leaving small numbered cards at areas of interest, photographing everything.

Ryan left the first body and entered the lounge, his DS following close behind.

The mother lay crumpled on the floor, facedown, one arm stretched out in the direction of the doorway Ryan had just walked through. The back of her t-shirt was dark with blood, so much so that it was difficult to tell what colour it had been originally, and her blonde hair was also dyed red with blood.

Pixello's voice came from behind them. "Like I said, nasty business."

"The child was on the stairs," Ryan said, thinking out loud. "Had she been running away? Running up to her bedroom, perhaps? It would be a natural safe space for a child."

"She'd have been better off running for the front door and the road outside, where she might have actually got help from someone," Pixello said.

Kids didn't think that way.

"She didn't run to her mother, which makes me think the mother was killed first. Perhaps Elizabeth shouted to Kiera to run and hide while she was being stabbed. Otherwise, the daughter's first instinct would have been to run to her mum for help."

"The husband going missing doesn't look good on him," Pixello said. "But there's no obvious motive, that we're aware of yet. Everyone we've spoken to says they were a normal, happy family."

Ryan pursed his lips. "That doesn't mean the husband isn't responsible, though. Plenty of people have different lives behind closed doors."

Was there such a thing as a normal family? Everyone had their secrets, didn't they? His own homelife was hardly anything to write home about. He and his wife, Donna, had been growing more and more distant ever since their daughter, Hayley, had been born. Not that he blamed Hayley in the slightest—he would never wish her out of his life—but they'd struggled over her baby years, with all the sleepless nights and the stress that had come from the constant crying that had filled their home. Any fun had been sucked out of their marriage, and they'd started blaming each other for never doing enough. It was a fair point from Donna's side—he'd been out at work, leaving her to deal with the baby alone for long hours. Her mother had been there more than he had. But what was he supposed to have done about that—quit? That was never going to happen, and she'd known he was also married to the job. Perhaps there hadn't just been three people in their family, the job had made it four, and it was too much.

It wasn't as though he didn't love her anymore, or even that he didn't fancy her—'cause he definitely did, and he hoped she felt the same way about him. He didn't think he was too bad to look at, even though he was in his forties now, and his dark hair had long been doused with a good shake of salt and pepper. He wasn't as lean as he'd been in his twenties, or even early thirties either, something that wasn't helped by his love of a good steak and a couple of beers on a Saturday night. He'd even joined a local football club and had a kickabout on a Wednesday evening when he wasn't working, but the middle-aged spread probably would only be held back by several intense gym sessions a week, and he didn't have the time nor inclination to be bothered by any of that crap.

No, his marriage was suffering more from a case of tiredness, boredom, and a feeling of 'is this as good as it's going to get?' But he didn't want to break up his family, and he hoped his wife felt the same way.

He turned his attention back to the case. "You said we haven't found the murder weapon yet?"

"No, we haven't, though it would seem as though a knife was used."

"Have you checked the knife block in the kitchen, see if one's missing?" DS Swift asked.

"Yes, but they're all in place. There might have been one in a drawer that could have been taken, though. We'll know more about the kind of knife that was used once the post-mortem has been done."

A knife used inside a house tended to mean a domestic killing. It was where most murders of women took place after all. There was a reason why they tended to look towards the husband or boyfriend first when this kind of thing happened; it wasn't lazy police work, it was simply the most likely option. Too many men thinking they had the right over a woman's life. Unfortunately, murders like this one that took place inside the home also carried a much lower sentence than if it had happened out on the street. It wasn't something Ryan agreed with, but he was there to catch the bad guys, not decide their punishment, though sometimes he would have liked to.

"Keep going," he instructed. "Make sure we search the outside of the property, too, in case the killer dumped it on the way out."

The sergeant nodded. "Already on it."

Not having the murder weapon always made his job harder. If they had it, they could dust for prints. Without it, they were left trying to decipher the prints left every day in a busy family home from those of a potential killer. Plus, if the husband *was* responsible, his prints would be all over this place anyway, and it wouldn't prove a thing.

"I'll go and see if the uniformed officers have found any decent witnesses," Erica said. "Someone might have seen something."

"Find out about the family dynamic as well," Ryan told her. "See if anyone heard the couple fighting, either today or at any other time."

"Will do, boss."

He paused for a moment as she headed for the front door and then turned back to the sergeant.

"What about other family?" Ryan asked Pixello. "Have any of them been informed yet?"

"Not yet. As far as our initial enquiries go, the husband's family are all dead, and the wife only has her mother who is in a care home."

"Has anyone broken the news to her yet?"

Pixello pressed his lips together and shook his head. "Not yet. We're not sure how much she understands."

That poor woman. What a fucking tragic way to end a life.

Where the hell was Douglas Lloyd? He checked his phone quickly to see if he'd missed a call from Lauren Fortum to say that the dogs had caught a trail and were closing in on the missing driver, but there was nothing.

If Lloyd had done this—murdered his family, run, and crashed the car—he couldn't have made it far from the crash site without help. But there had been no reports of sightings of a badly injured man, and no one had been brought into hospital matching his description or the description of the injuries he would most likely have sustained. If he'd called someone to pick him up, he would have had some difficult questions to answer.

Unless Ryan was going down the wrong track and the husband wasn't the one who'd killed his family.

Chapter Five

With DI Chase inside the house, Erica turned her attention to finding some witnesses. A family doesn't get murdered in the middle of the day in a busy neighbourhood without someone hearing or seeing something. The neighbours were all either standing by their front doors or peering through their front-room windows, trying to get an idea of what was going on.

One woman in particular seemed upset, the sleeve of her longline cardigan bunched up in her hand and held to her face. A uniformed officer was already speaking to her, so Erica approached.

"I'm DS Swift," she introduced herself. "I wondered if I could have a word?"

The woman's gaze flicked between herself and the uniformed officer, who smiled and nodded, and stepped back to give Erica room.

"I assume you're their direct neighbour?" Erica asked the woman.

"Yes, I am. I've lived next door for almost seven years now. I can't believe this has happened. Who would do something so terrible to Beth and poor little Keira? She was such a sweetheart. I'd have her round to play if they needed to pop out or something."

"You knew them well then, Mrs...?" She trailed off to allow the other woman to fill in the gap.

"Pincher. Maeve Pincher. And yes, I'd say I did. We've had barbecues round at each other's houses and that sort of thing."

"Would you say you were more friends than neighbours?"

"Yes, I would." She pressed her knuckles to her lips. "Poor little girl. How could anyone do such a thing. Everyone round here is saying it was Doug, but I don't believe it for a second."

"Douglas Lloyd?"

"That's right.

"Did you know Douglas well?"

"Not as well as I knew his wife and daughter. I mean, he wasn't around as much because he works away a lot with his job. Besides, he's a man, and men always keep stuff back, don't they? Women will just talk about everything."

Erica cocked her head to one side. "Did you get the feeling he was keeping secrets?"

She started back. "No, I didn't mean it like that." She lowered her voice slightly. "He did like a bit of a flutter on the odd occasion, though, mainly on the scratch cards, I think. He came home a few times grinning from ear to ear 'cause he'd had a win."

"He was a gambler then?"

"Well, yes, but not in a bad way. I think it was just a way of passing the time. A hobby. I don't think he would have got in any bad way with it, if that's what you're thinking."

"We need to keep all possibilities open right now."

If he liked to gamble, there was the chance he owed money to the wrong people. Perhaps they'd come to the house to threaten the family as a way of making him pay up, only for things to have gone wrong.

"What about his wife and daughter?" Erica asked. "Did they ever seem frightened of him? Did you ever hear them fighting or anything like that?"

"No, not at all, at least no more than any other couple. We all have rows, don't we? It's just a normal part of being married. Did you find Douglas then? He wasn't in the house?"

"No, we haven't located Mr Lloyd yet. I don't suppose you happened to see when he left. Is Douglas normally the one who drives the car?" There was no car on the driveway for the property.

"No, it's the family car that's missing. He has a company car, the BMW that's parked on the street over there." She pointed to a slick, dark-grey BMW 5 Series. "Beth just has an old silver Ford. I can't even remember what type it is now."

She shook her head at her bad memory, but it didn't matter. Erica didn't say that she could tell her exactly which Ford model Elizabeth Lloyd had driven, and even its number plate.

"He has a company car? Do you know what he works as?"

Maeve flapped a hand. "Something to do with sales. He's away a lot for work. I'm not entirely sure. It's not exactly an interesting topic of conversation, is it?"

"It could be important," she pressed.

"Yes, I suppose it could be, but I really can't remember. Sorry."

"That's okay. Can you think about earlier today? When did you last see the car on the driveway?"

"Umm...I'm not totally sure, but it was definitely here this afternoon."

"What about when Douglas went to work? What time does he leave?"

"He normally heads out about eightish, sometimes earlier."

"Did you see him leave this morning?" Erica asked.

Maeve twisted her lips. "I don't think so."

"And what about later? Did you notice him come home again?"

Maeve shook her head. "No, and I definitely would have remembered if I had. He wouldn't usually get back until much later. Half past six or even seven o'clock, on the days he does come home."

That could be important. If he came home earlier than normal, there would be a reason behind that. Someone might have contacted him to say there was a problem and he was needed at home. Would that have been the wife or someone else? If it was someone else, it might be the same person who'd killed them, assuming it wasn't the husband, of course. Or perhaps he'd discovered something he hadn't liked and had come home in a fit of rage and murdered his wife and daughter? Until they knew for certain how many people had been in the crashed car, they were just guessing.

Erica continued to question the neighbour.

"What about Elizabeth and Keira? Did you see them at any point during the day?"

"I waved from the window when Beth walked Keira to school. That would have been about half past eight. I generally see them again at about half past three, quarter to four, when they're on their way home, but I was on a phone call, so I wasn't paying much attention."

The mother and daughter had been murdered sometime between coming home from school, at three-thirty, and the car being found by the boys after five. That didn't give the killer much time. She made a mental note to check with the school to make sure Kiera Lloyd didn't leave early for any reason.

The car was found about thirty minutes away from here. Did the killer have time to come back once the girl had finished school, kill the family, then run, and crash the car and flee the scene? It wouldn't have given them long, and they'd have been covered in blood. Someone must have seen them.

"One final question, Mrs Pincher, though we may need to speak to you again later. Did you notice anyone unusual hanging around the house? Any strange cars on the street?"

Her face crumpled. "No, I don't think so. I'm sorry I can't be of more help."

"You've been lots of help." She handed the neighbour her card. "But if you think of anything else, don't hesitate to call."

Chapter Six

Michelle Mabry glanced at her watch. It was Friday evening, and her husband Russell was normally home by now. He spent the week away for work, travelling around the country, so she hadn't seen him since he'd left Monday morning. She'd spoken to him last night though, as he'd done his customary call home to speak to her and their son, and he hadn't made any mention of being late today. She'd already phoned him a couple of times, but there was no answer; it just went straight through to his answer phone.

A thunder of feet came down the stairs, and her son ran into the room.

She sighed in irritation. "Max, I thought I'd told you to change out of your school uniform. I need to put it in the wash."

Max peered down at his t-shirt, embroidered with the school logo at the breast, as though he'd completely forgotten he was wearing it. At seven years old, and with a mind and body that barely seemed capable of focusing on one thing for more than thirty seconds, he probably had.

"Oh yeah. I'll do it in a minute. Is Dad home yet? He promised me he'd buy me some more Robux when he got back."

Michelle sighed again. "You spend too much time on that computer game. You should be outside, playing or riding your bike."

"You want me to go out in the dark?"

She blinked up at the window. How had it got dark so early? She was sure it had only been five o'clock ten minutes ago. Now it was already evening, and she hadn't even started dinner yet.

Come on, Russ. Where the hell are you?

"How about we order pizza?" she asked her son, trying to distract him.

"Tonight? But we normally have a takeaway on Saturday with a film on the TV."

"Yeah, well, silly Mummy forgot to get the mince out of the freezer, so we'll have it tonight instead. Unless you'd rather go hungry, of course?"

His eyes widened. "No way!"

Being hungry was one thing that did not go over well with Max. Even at his age, he could eat the same size portion as she did. She couldn't imagine what it was going to be like feeding him when he became a teenager. She was going to need to take out a second mortgage to be able to afford to feed him.

"Where *is* Dad?" Max asked again.

Michelle had the feeling Max was more concerned about getting his money to spend on his computer game than any actual concern for the whereabouts of his father.

She sighed. "Go and get your tablet, and I'll see if I can figure out how to put the Robux on your account for you."

Max punched the air. "Yes! Thanks, Mum. You're the best."

He ran off to retrieve the tablet.

She took the quiet moment to call Russell's mobile again. Once more, it rang and rang. "You know who it is," his voice said down the line. "Leave a message, and I'll get back to you as soon as I can."

"It's me again. You were supposed to be home over an hour ago. Can you call me, please? I'm getting worried."

She chewed at her thumbnail. It wasn't as though he worked in an office and went out for drinks after work or anything like that. Sometimes he was late, especially if he'd had to make a call several counties over and had got stuck in traffic, but he always called her to let her know.

Max reappeared and shoved his tablet at her, demanding her attention. "Here you go, Mum."

"You're going to need to show me what to do."

"You just put in the password. I've already done everything else."

It amazed her how computer literate kids were these days. "Okay, give it here then." She carried her son's tablet over to the sofa.

At least she knew what the password was. Even though she was aware that you were supposed to have different ones for all the different sites, as a family, they tended to have a variation of the same one.

The buzz of her phone caught her attention, and she dropped the tablet to snatch it up. *Russell?*

But no, it was Caroline, one of the other mums from school. She let out a sigh and swiped to ignore the call. She didn't need to get caught up in a gossipy chat right now. But what if Caroline knew something about Russ's whereabouts, and that was why she was calling? What if he'd been in an accident, and Caroline was phoning because she'd spotted his car or something?

She picked up the phone again and swiped to bring up the last action.

"Muuuum," Max whined, shoving the tablet back at her. She still hadn't put the password in.

"In a minute, Max," she snapped.

The phone rang, and Caroline picked up. "Oh, hi. I just wondered if you knew if Taekwondo was on tomorrow?"

The Saturday class both their boys attended.

"What?" Michelle's head was spinning. Why was Caroline asking her about bloody Taekwondo?

"I couldn't remember if it was this week that the instructor said he was on holiday? I don't suppose you know?"

"No, no, I'm sorry, I don't. I really have to go, Caroline, sorry." She ended the call again, threw her phone back down and put her head in her hands. Was she overreacting? He was only a couple of hours late now. But in her gut, she knew something had happened to him.

Max nudged the tablet back at her. "The password, Mum."

"Jesus Christ, there are more important things than your damned computer game!" she shouted.

Max stared, wide-eyed at her outburst, and she burst into tears.

Chapter Seven

"How did you get on?" Ryan asked Erica as he left the house and approached his sergeant outside.

She pressed her lips together, her forehead knotted in a frown. "I haven't found anyone who even saw what time Douglas Lloyd left the house this afternoon, but I have narrowed down the time of death to being between three-thirty, when they got back from school, and five p.m. That only gives whoever was driving the family car thirty minutes to get across the city and crash the car."

"In rush-hour traffic?" he said. "I'd say we can narrow it down even more than that."

"You think the attack must have happened sometime between three-thirty and four-thirty?"

Ryan nodded. "An hour is a good window for us to narrow things down further. With any luck, one of the neighbours' houses will have CCTV or video camera doorbells. Someone must have seen something. A woman and child won't have been murdered in the middle of the day, in a busy housing estate, without someone having seen something."

"One of the neighbours, Maeve Pincher, mentioned that the BMW over there is Douglas Lloyd's company car. We should have it searched, too."

"Good spot." Ryan chewed at a piece of dried skin on his lower lip. "I wonder why he took the wife's car rather than that one?"

"Not sure." She shrugged one shoulder. "If it was even him who took the car at all. If someone else was responsible and needed to make a quick getaway, they would have just taken whichever car they found the keys for."

"Or it was a way to throw us off the scent. If he took his own company car to escape in, we would be more likely to pin this on him."

"Maybe." Erica glanced back over her shoulder to where the neighbours were still being held back by uniformed officers. "There was something else the neighbour mentioned. She said Douglas like to have the occasional flutter on the scratch cards."

"Is that right? I wonder if it was more than that?"

"That's what I thought. If he had gambling issues, perhaps there were also money worries. Maybe he borrowed from the wrong people and this was their revenge."

Ryan thought for a moment. "The PCN check came back clean, though. I'd expect someone with problems of that level to have some kind of background. This guy doesn't have so much as a parking ticket."

Erica raised her eyebrows. "They always say it's the quiet ones you need to watch out for."

"Hmm, maybe. We mustn't lose sight of the possibility that Douglas Lloyd is a victim in all of this as well, though. Until we find a murder weapon with his prints on it, we can't know for sure."

"Any sign of it yet?" she asked.

"Not yet, but it can't just have vanished. There's a chance we'll find it around the woodland near the car, if the killer took it with them."

"That's a much bigger area to cover."

"It doesn't help that we're out of daylight either. The dogs might have found something, but if not, it'll have to be resumed in the morning."

Ryan stifled a yawn. He was tired, and it was well past his official knocking off time, but he wouldn't be going home yet. There was still far too much work to be done.

Movement came from the front door of the house. "Detective," a male voice called.

Ryan turned to see the lead Scenes of Crime Officer standing there. "What did you find?"

He held up a clear evidence bag containing a phone—a Samsung of some kind. "A mobile phone hidden in the house."

Ryan left Erica and walked back up the path to the house. "Where was it?"

"Taped down the back of the husband's sock drawer."

That perked Ryan up. Decent husbands didn't need to hide mobile phones in their own homes. "I assume it's locked."

"You assume correctly."

"Get it to Digital Forensics. They should be able to get it unlocked."

Would the reason a man would kill his own family be on that phone?

He went back to Erica to discover her on the phone. She lifted her hand to him and mouthed *Fortum*. He gave her a minute to finish the call, hoping that whatever Fortum had to say, it was positive.

"Any news from the other crime scene?" he asked when she'd finished.

"Not yet. They're still searching. The dogs picked up a scent but only managed to follow it to the road, and then it vanished."

"He might have been picked up then. Dogs don't lose a trail unless something drastic has happened like the person they're tracking gets into a vehicle."

Erica nodded. "Yes, but by who?"

"The same person he's been calling on the secret mobile?" Of course, Lloyd might not have been able to call that person if he didn't have the phone, unless he had a backup. "People tend not to conceal phones in their own homes unless they're hiding something.

"Something to do with the gambling, perhaps?"

"Possibly. We'll know more once we get it open."

"I want to interview the boys in more detail," Erica said. "The younger of the two seemed anxious earlier."

"That's hardly surprising, considering what they found."

"Maybe, but it's an instinct, and I think it would be best to speak to them while everything is fresh in their minds. I was going to swing by and pick up Liam and his mother on the way back to the station."

"Okay. Get DC Penn to pick up the other one." They had several detective constables in the team, and he intended on making use of them. "It's probably best we keep them apart until we get the chance to speak to them properly."

Erica gave a curt nod. "Agreed."

Chapter Eight

Erica stopped outside of the Vulnerable Interview Suite where Liam Gilbert sat inside with his mother. She keyed in the code on the pad on the outside of the door, waited until it buzzed to tell her it was open, and then stepped inside. They both fixed their attention on her as she entered, and she pasted on a smile.

"Sorry to keep you waiting."

Marie Gilbert shook her head. "It's okay. We know you're busy."

"Have you got everything you need? You're comfortable?" Erica asked.

Liam's mother shot a look to her son and then offered him a smile. "Yes, we're fine. Thank you. Just keen to get home, you know. It's getting late."

Erica had stopped by the Gilbert household on her way back from the second crime scene. Marie Gilbert was right, it was getting late, so late in fact, that Erica had needed to phone her husband, Chris. He wouldn't be happy that she wouldn't be making it home for dinner that night, and most likely wouldn't be home for bedtime either. She hated missing Poppy's bedtimes, but what could she do? It wasn't as though she could just pretend there hadn't been a double murder and the husband—and current main suspect—was missing.

"Yes, of course. I'll try to be as quick as I can. I do have some questions to ask you, Liam, and we do have microphones in the room to record what I'm asking you and what your responses are. It just helps us when we go back over what's been said. I'd say I'd write it all down instead, but my handwriting is terrible, and I can never read it."

The boy's lips tweaked in a smile. "My handwriting is terrible, too."

"Well, you've got plenty of years left in school to improve yours. I'm afraid I'm a lost cause."

That won her a wider smile.

"So," she sat in the comfortable chair opposite, "let's start earlier that day, shall we? What did you do after you got up this morning?"

Liam shrugged. "I went to school, like I always do."

"And how is school? Do you enjoy it?"

"It's all right. I like my friends and playing football at lunchtime."

"Friends like Conner?"

He ducked his head as he nodded and didn't meet her eye. "Yeah, friends like Conner."

"Then what happened after school was over?" she asked.

"Conner said we should hang out, so we did."

His mother interrupted, hurriedly. "The boys often hang out after school. So long as they're back before dark, we let them have their independence. I mean, they're going to secondary school later this year, so they need to learn how to be on their own a bit more. I do think we mollycoddle kids these days, and I'd rather they were outside than sitting in, playing on their computer games."

It was clear Marie was worried about her parenting being judged. That was the last thing Erica was going to do. She had a baby at home who was mostly being taken care of by her husband, not that there should be anything wrong with that in this day and age. Chris was Poppy's father, after all, but she still felt as though people thought there was something wrong with her for not wanting to be at home with her daughter and instead being out catching criminals.

"Oh, I agree," she said instead. "It's good for boys to burn off some energy."

The woman's shoulders dropped, and she smiled. "Yes, they're a bit like dogs. Feed them and walk them and they'll be fine." Her cheeks flushed. "Not that I'm calling my son a dog," she added.

"No, of course not." Erica turned her attention back to Liam. "So, you finished school, but I noticed you weren't wearing your school clothes earlier. Did you change?"

"Yeah, we both went home and got changed and then came out again."

"You were quite a long way from home—almost two miles, actually. Is that a normal distance for you to walk?"

He glanced down at his lap. "I suppose. We don't really keep track."

The mother stepped in again. "I'd rather they walked through the fields than hung out on the estate. I know there's fewer people around, but it feels safer."

"Of course. I just wanted to make sure that this was normal for the boys and they hadn't altered their route for any reason."

Marie's eyes widened. "You mean in case someone wanted them to find the car?"

"I'd say that's highly unlikely, but we have to take all these things into consideration."

"I didn't want to go into the woods," Liam said, "but Conner did. He said we could cut through and then go to the shop down the road and he'd buy us some sweets."

"It was Conner's idea then?"

DC Penn was interviewing the other boy. The interviews were being recorded to compare later to make sure the boys' stories matched. Erica got the impression from Liam that Conner was the ringleader out of the two, but that might have been Liam trying to push the blame onto his friend.

"Maybe. It was getting dark, and I didn't want Mum to worry." He shot his mother a look, and she reached out and patted the back of his hand.

"Okay, tell me a little about what happened when you found the car. Who saw it first, you or Conner?"

"It was Conner, I think. I noticed where the tree and bushes were all flattened from where the car must have come off the road, but the car was to our left and almost behind us, so I didn't see that until after Conner spotted it."

"Do you remember seeing anyone else around at the time? Or hearing anyone or anything?"

He shook his head. "No, nothing. It was just the two of us."

"You're doing really well," she encouraged him. "We're nearly done. After you saw the car, who approached it first?"

"Conner did," he said with certainty. "I was worried it might blow up—" his mother sucked in a sharp breath and closed her eyes briefly, clearly picturing that exact thing happening—"but it didn't, so I walked up to where Conner was standing at the door."

"The driver's door, or the passenger door?" she checked.

He wrinkled his forehead as he thought. "The passenger door."

"And this is really important, Liam. Do you remember if the doors were open or shut when you got there?"

"Umm, I think it was shut, but it might have been open a little bit."

"Is there any way Conner might have touched the door while you weren't looking? Perhaps pushed it shut, or anything like that?"

"No, I don't think so. We didn't touch anything."

Her gaze flitted to her notes "That's not quite true, is it, Liam? When we spoke to you at the scene, you said you put your hands against the glass, cupping your face so you could see inside better."

His cheeks reddened, and she saw the resemblance to his mother.

"Oh, yeah. We just wanted to make sure there was no one hurt inside."

"It's okay. You're not in any trouble. It's just important for us to get the real picture about what happened in the time leading up to the car being found, and sometimes it's those little details that can make the big difference in finding out what happened to the driver."

"Do you think he's dead?"

"I'm afraid we simply don't have that information, Liam."

The boy nodded.

"The car they found," Marie said, chewing on her lower lip, "it was linked to that other...thing...that happened in the city today, wasn't it?"

Erica gave her a polite smile. "I'm sorry, I can't disclose that information."

"No, of course not. I'm sorry, I shouldn't have asked."

"Not a problem." Erica glanced back down at her notes. "Now, where were we?" Unfortunately, she wasn't going to let them go so soon. "How about we just go back over what happened when you first saw the car?"

ERICA OPENED HER FRONT door with the key in the lock, moving slowly and carefully in the hope of not waking anyone up. Sometimes it could take hours to get Poppy settled, and she knew her husband, Chris, wouldn't appreciate it if he'd just got her to sleep only for Erica to come home and wake her up again.

Truthfully, Erica also didn't want to deal with trying to get Poppy back down again either, and she experienced a twang of guilt at the thought. That poor mother and daughter at the house today. The mother must have put her daughter to bed last night, possibly having the same thoughts, overtired and stressed and just wanting an hour to herself, completely unaware that it would be the last time she'd ever get to kiss her daughter goodnight. Erica blinked back a sudden prick of tears and sucked in a breath. She'd been in this job a good few years now but hadn't figured out how to switch off the empathy button just yet. Maybe that was a good thing.

She closed the door softly behind her and tiptoed into the kitchen, dropping her bag, shrugging off her jacket, and kicking away her shoes as she went. She flicked on the kitchen light. Chris had left her a note.

Dinner in the microwave. C. X

She pushed the button and opened the microwave door. Sure enough, sitting on a plate and covered in cling film was a portion of lasagne. He was too good to her. She put it on to warm through and went to the fridge and poured herself a glass of white wine from the bottle that was already open. She took a good gulp, and the microwave pinged to signal her food was ready.

Erica ate standing up at the kitchen worktop, barely even tasting what she was eating. She savoured the wine a little more but knew she needed to go to bed and get some sleep. This new case was a big one, and they needed as many bodies on the job as possible which meant an early start.

An arm wrapped around her waist, and she held back a scream.

She twisted in her husband's arms. "Bloody hell, Chris. You scared the shit out of me. I didn't hear you come in."

He only wore the boxer shorts he slept in, his bare chest warm from being in bed. "Sorry. I wasn't exactly quiet."

Erica let out a shaky breath. "It's my fault. I was completely lost in thought."

"About the case?" he asked.

"Yeah, it was a mother and daughter killed. The husband is missing. We don't know if it was someone else responsible or him yet."

"Shit, that's horrible. I don't know how you do it."

She smiled. "Having a good man at home helps."

Chris wasn't only a house husband; he also ran his own business designing websites and doing other internet-based things that she didn't quite understand. He'd gone part time since Poppy had been born, and she'd gone back to work full time, and he never complained about trying to balance the two.

He leaned in and kissed her. "Glad to hear it. Now can I take you up to bed?"

"Absolutely. I'm shattered." She tried not to react to the disappointed look on his face. "Just give me five minutes to finish up here and go and give Poppy a kiss goodnight."

"Don't wake her," Chris warned over his shoulder as he turned from her to leave the kitchen.

"I won't."

She finished her wine and stacked the glass and her empty plate in the dishwasher, then went up to the bathroom and cleaned her teeth. Then she sneaked into her daughter's bedroom. A nightlight effused the corner of the room in a warm yellow glow, and her gaze went to the cot that held the sleeping form of her daughter. Her little arms were splayed either side of her head, her lips parted in her sleep. The baby sleeping bag covered her feet and torso, and she'd kicked off the extra blanket Chris had tucked around her when he'd put her to bed. Her special toy—a little white bunny with a blanket attached to it—had fallen halfway through the bars, so Erica picked it up and tucked it in closer to Poppy's cheek.

I'll never let anything or anyone hurt you, she silently swore to herself.

"Goodnight baby-girl," she whispered. "I love you."

Chapter Nine

DI Ryan Chase got into the office early. There hadn't been any developments overnight, and Douglas Lloyd still hadn't been located. They had a busy day ahead of them, and he intended to call a briefing the minute everyone else arrived.

"Did you manage to get some sleep?" he asked DS Swift as she dumped her bag down beside her desk.

She nodded. "A few hours."

He imagined she'd been much like him, awake early, mind racing, aware that things needed to be done, and that wasn't happening while they were lying around.

He hadn't seen Donna when he'd got home last night. It had been late, and everyone had already been in bed, much as he'd expected. He'd hovered outside their bedroom door, listening for any signs that his wife might still be awake, but if she was, she'd done her best to pretend she wasn't. In the end, deciding it was best if he didn't wake her, he took himself into their spare room. He was knackered and would probably snore his head off, which would only make things tenser between the two of them. He'd set his alarm for five, aware he could get by on that amount of sleep, but then had needed to check that he'd set it for the right time several times over. Sometimes it was impossible to silence that niggling thought in his head, insisting that he'd pressed the wrong button and would sleep right through it refusing to leave until he'd done so. He told himself it was because he needed to be in early—which he did—but there was also a part of him that knew he was avoiding Donna. He'd made sure to nip into Hayley's bedroom before he'd left, giving her a kiss and a cuddle and tucking her back in again. She'd probably get up and crawl into her mother's bed earlier than normal, but they'd most likely both fall back to sleep again. It was a Saturday, after all.

There was no such thing as weekends for a detective when there was a big case on.

"Any progress overnight?" Erica asked. "I see the husband still hasn't been located."

Ryan dragged his hand over the top of his head. "Nope. The son of a bitch has vanished into thin air."

"Or he's been snatched and is a victim in all of this as well."

"Perhaps, but that hidden phone doesn't exactly put him in a good light."

"True, but just because he has secrets doesn't automatically make him capable of killing his wife and daughter."

Ryan offered her a dry smile. "You think far too highly of people, Swift. Give it another few years, and you'll be a dried-up old pessimist like me."

"You must have at least a couple of decades on me, sir," she said, teasing him.

"Funny." He jerked his chin towards the briefing room. "We'd better get in there."

His boss, DCI Mandy Hirst, was already in the room. She was a serious, compact woman in her fifties with short grey hair and sharp, light-blue eyes behind her glasses.

One wall had been covered with the photographs of the two victims' bodies, a head shot of Douglas Lloyd, together with several shots of the car—exterior and interior—and a map pinpointing the distance between where they were all found. He pressed his lips together and shook his head at the images. No one should have their lives ended in such a brutal way.

"Good morning, DI Chase." The DCI didn't smile. "DS Swift. I'm expecting a busy day so we can make some progress on this case. I don't like having two murder victims and no one under arrest yet."

Ryan nodded. "We should have reports from the pathologist and hopefully from forensics as well by the end of the day."

There were effectively two crime scenes that were being processed—the house and the car. There was no doubt in Ryan's mind that the two were linked, but getting confirmation that the blood inside the car was Douglas Lloyd's would help to solidify the pattern of events. Had he acted alone? Was the blood due to the car accident, or had he been injured before he'd got behind the wheel—if it was even him who'd been driving?

News got round of the early morning briefing, and gradually the rest of his team filed in and found seats.

DCI Hirst stood up. "Good morning, everyone. We have another busy day ahead of us. I'd like to think we'll have someone in custody by the end of the day so don't let me down. Now, I'll hand you over to DI Chase."

Ryan took up his position at the front of the room and did a roll call for each of his team members and then looked to his sergeant.

"You conducted an interview with one of the boys, Liam Gilbert, yesterday evening?" he checked.

"That's right," Erica said, "and DC Penn spoke with Conner Lowry. Both their stories match up, and they're both saying the doors were shut when they found the car, which means whoever was inside was well enough to not only open a door to get out, but then bothered to shut it behind them. This means, assuming Douglas Lloyd was even inside the car, he was clearly not badly injured enough to prevent him making a getaway or else someone else closed the door and helped Lloyd."

DC Mallory Lawson, one of the detective constables, stood. "We have a neighbour who says she saw the family car, a silver Ford Focus estate, pull out of the drive at about four-thirty. The car was then found about a thirty-minute drive away at five-thirty. Which means we have a window of half an hour where whoever was driving crashed and then escaped and abandoned the vehicle."

"Did the neighbour happen to see who was driving, or how many people were in the car?" Ryan asked.

"Unfortunately not. She just noticed the vehicle reverse out of the drive."

Ryan paced from one side of the room to the other as he spoke. "I want all CCTV footage between five and five-thirty of the roads around the accident site. We must have caught the car before the accident. And if a second car was involved in getting him away from the crash site, we could have that, too."

"We still don't have a murder weapon yet," Erica added, "and we're still waiting on Digital Forensics to crack a phone that was found hidden in the house. Reports are that Douglas Lloyd liked to gamble, but whether or not that has anything to do with what's happened to his wife and daughter is yet unclear."

Ryan nodded. "I want us to speak to everyone close to the family, including any friends or relatives. Find out if there's anything behind the gambling rumours. Right now, CCTV is going to give us our best lead. We believe a vehicle must have picked up Lloyd since the dogs lost his scent suddenly on the road. If we can find that car, we can find him. Let's not end the day until we do."

He made sure everyone knew what actions they needed to take and ended the meeting. Before he left the room, he checked DCI Hirst was happy with the lines of enquiry they were following, and then he went back to his desk. He logged on to his computer to see the coroner's report had come in on the mother and daughter. It made for grim reading. Elizabeth Lloyd had been stabbed three times in the stomach with a serrated blade approximately five inches in length. She'd died from the resulting blood loss leading to heart failure. Her daughter hadn't been stabbed but had been suffocated. From the bruising on her face, it would seem a large hand placed over her mouth and nose had been all it had taken. Neither of the victims had been sexually assaulted. Blood and skin cells had been retrieved from beneath both the mother and daughter's fingernails which indicated that they'd fought back. Forensics were processing the findings to see if the DNA matched that of Douglas Lloyd's or any DNA that had been found in the car.

Someone approached his desk, and he lifted his head to see one of the young detective constables, Mallory Lawson, standing there. Mallory was in her twenties and had an alternative look for a police officer, which she toned down for work. There were several holes in her face—her nose, under her lip, and in her ears—that spoke of piercings that had been removed at some point, and he was pretty sure she hid a number of tattoos under her work suit. He had no idea what her natural hair colour was, but right now it was dyed jet-black and shaved underneath the longer upper layer. She made him feel like a dinosaur.

"Boss, I thought you'd want to know that we have the CCTV footage back from the shop that's a mile down the road. It catches the Lloyd's Ford driving past at seventeen-oh-three, but it's impossible to make out who's in the car. I've sent it over to see if someone can blow up the images some more, but I don't have my hopes up on that."

"What about other cars that drove past?" he asked. "Have we got some licence plates? One of them might have stopped to pick up the driver."

"Yes, several. It might be a quiet road normally, but at that time in the evening, with everyone coming home from work, it wasn't. The CCTV has recorded forty-one cars driving between the time our car went past and the boys finding the accident."

He blew out his cheeks in frustration. Forty-one cars and drivers were going to take some time to work their way through. The more time it took them, the harder it was going to be to track down Douglas Lloyd.

"Can you and DC Penn follow up on each of these licence plates and speak to whoever was behind the wheel at the time. Even if we can't find whoever picked up the two injured people, we might find someone who saw something but didn't bother to report it. You know how people like to convince themselves whatever they saw was nothing because that's easier than going to the trouble of calling it in."

"Or they go the other way and report every tiny thing and have their noses in everyone else's business," she commented.

Ryan rolled his eyes. "I'm not sure which one's worse."

Chapter Ten

Michelle had barely slept all night and instead had lain awake listening for the sound of the door opening and Russell's feet on the stairs as his made his way up to bed. She tried his mobile phone number for the hundredth time, but it went straight to answer phone. There was no point in leaving a message—she'd already left numerous ones all saying the same thing. Who could she call who might know where he was? She didn't even have the numbers of any of his friends, and he didn't do social media, so it wasn't as though she could track any of them down from there. Besides, Russell didn't really have many close friends, not people he saw regularly, anyway. The people they hung out with tended to be her friends and their husbands or partners. He had the odd person he'd mention who he went to school with, but that was all. He'd even had her brother as his best man at their wedding. Perhaps she should have seen something strange in that, but she hadn't at the time, thinking instead that it was good of Russ for including her brother like that. He didn't have any family of his own, and the friends he had from school lived far away—one in Australia and the other in Hong Kong. Men weren't like women; they didn't have close friends. Not that she had many herself lately. There were some school mums she got on okay with, but she wouldn't exactly call them friends.

"Where's Dad?" Max asked, coming down the stairs in his pyjamas, rubbing sleep from his eyes. "Is he not home yet?"

"Oh, he had to stay away with work," she lied. "Now, who's hungry?"

She wanted to divert his attention, worried that if he asked too many questions, she might show her true feelings and only make him worried, too.

Max stuck his skinny arm in the air as though he was trying to answer a question at school. "Me, me!"

She ruffled his hair. "Good to hear it."

Normally, on a Saturday morning, she'd make the effort to cook something, but she was too distracted to focus on making pancakes or frying bacon today. Instead, she pulled out a box of cereal, a bowl, and some milk and let Max get stuck in.

She went to the living room and stood at the window, looking out onto the road at the front of the house, praying she would see Russ's car pull into the drive. She picked up her phone and checked it for a missed call, but there wasn't one. She tapped her fingers against her lips. Should she call the local hospital and see if anyone matching his description had been brought in, or even the police and report him as missing? A heavy weight had lodged itself into the middle of her chest, and her stomach churned. She hadn't been able to eat anything that morning and had barely managed a couple of sips of tea. Deep down, she was filled with that gnawing certainty that something huge had shifted in her world and from today, nothing was going to be the same.

When could she even call the police about a missing person? Was it twenty-four hours, or was that some bullshit myth people banded around? Had it even been twenty-four hours yet? When would they count that from considering Russell normally worked away, so it wasn't as though she'd actually seen him since Monday morning? Mentally, she calculated the last time she'd spoken to him. It had been Thursday evening, when he'd called to say goodnight to Max. She hadn't got the impression anything had been wrong then, but now she was doubting everything.

With her hand shaking, she searched up the number to call the local police station. This didn't feel like she should be calling nine-nine-nine, as it wasn't technically an emergency, was it? They'd probably just look at her with pity and comment how plenty of boyfriends and husbands didn't come home on a Friday night. They'd think he'd got drunk and picked up some woman and gone back to hers and would come crawling home sheepishly with a bad hangover and an apology. Despite knowing this, she still needed to call. She'd tell them how he wasn't like that, and how he'd never stayed out without letting her know where he was before.

She closed the lounge door quietly, hoping Max wouldn't notice or try to interrupt her. She thought he'd take the opportunity to sneak some time on his tablet, most likely hiding back under his covers in bed.

She looked up the non-emergency number, dialled, and the operator answered.

"Hello, I'd like to report a missing person." Her eyes filled with tears as she said the words out loud, and a painful lump choked her throat. "It's…it's my husband. He didn't come home last night after he finished work, and I haven't heard from him since." A tear escaped her eye and slid down her cheek.

"Could he be staying with family or a friend?"

"No, he doesn't have anyone."

"Okay, let me take some details. Let's start with his name."

She rattled off everything the call operator was asking her, the whole time praying Russell would show up and make her look like an idiot.

"Mrs Mabry, your husband isn't classed as a vulnerable person, so this won't be considered an emergency. I'll make a log of it, and I'll get a police officer to come around and speak to you in due course."

Flutters of panic danced in her chest. "Do you know when that will be?"

"Whenever we have someone free, Mrs Mabry. We're very busy."

She was getting the brush-off, that much was clear, but she wasn't going to give up that easily. In her mind, there was nothing normal about this situation. Nothing at all.

Chapter Eleven

Erica was at her desk when her phone rang.
She answered. "Swift."

"It's Mike Pembroke from Digital Forensics. Thought you'd want to know that we managed to get into the phone that was found at the Lloyd house."

Erica sat up straighter. "Did you find anything interesting?"

"The phone only has a few numbers on there, the majority of which appear to be unregistered. There was one number that was registered, however, to a Michelle Francis Mabry, and there are a number of missed calls and answerphone messages that have been left on the phone over the past twenty-four hours from the same person."

"Michelle Mabry?" she checked.

"Yes. From the messages, she seemed very concerned about the whereabouts of whoever it was she was trying to get hold of. She kept asking where he was and when he was coming home. I've emailed you the transcripts."

She clicked on the computer and brought them up. Sure enough, the messages were just the same thing, insistences that the owner of the phone call her, and asking where he was and when he'd be home.

"Those read like the messages of a worried wife to me," she said.

"I agree."

"What about the phone itself? Is it registered to anyone?"

"No, it's not. Sorry."

She fiddled with a pen on her desk. "No problem. Thanks for sending all of that over. At least we have one name to work with."

She hung up and then ran a check on the name Michelle Francis Mabry. She didn't have any kind of criminal background.

"Why were you calling a phone found in the home of a murdered family?" Erica asked out loud, addressing a woman she didn't yet know.

She searched other records for the name. Michelle was married to a Russell Mabry, but there was surprisingly little to be found about either of them online. Neither of them appeared to be on social media, though she found a marriage certificate, and they were both on the electoral roll, so she had an address. It was a local Bristol one.

Her curiosity deepened. She'd have considered that Michelle Mabry had been phoning the wrong number, but the number was stored in the phone under 'Michelle' as well.

Could the phone have been nicked and hidden in the house because it was stolen goods? It wasn't as though it was a particularly expensive phone, though.

Erica printed off the transcripts and took them over to Ryan's desk.

"Thought you might be interested in this," she told him. "Digital Forensics cracked the phone found in the Lloyd house."

She ran him through her thoughts and what had been discussed with Mike Pembroke.

Ryan sat back and tapped his pen against his teeth. Erica watched as he drummed a rhythm; *one, two, three, pause. One, two, three, pause.*

"There's one easy way to get to the bottom of this." He picked up his own phone. "Let's give Michelle Mabry a call and see if she knows why her husband's phone was hidden inside another woman's husband's sock drawer."

Chapter Twelve

Michelle thought she was going to lose her mind. It was the afternoon now, but she still hadn't heard anything from Russell, and the police hadn't been to see her either. She felt so utterly helpless. She'd called round everyone she knew, praying one of them had heard something from him. Her sister had been worried but had done her best to reassure her. She knew what everyone was thinking, though—that he'd done something stupid and didn't want to face the music. None of her friends and family knew Russell the way she did. Because he was away so much with work, they'd never really had the opportunity to get to know him properly.

Max had gone unusually quiet as well, and she could tell he was worried about his dad, even if he didn't say so out loud. He was normally a boisterous and happy boy, but today he'd hidden in his room, only coming down for snacks or to ask when his dad was coming home.

Suddenly, her phone buzzed beside her. She didn't recognise the number, but maybe it was her husband calling from someone else's phone. If he'd lost his, it would explain why he hadn't been answering any of her calls, though his phone had been going straight through to answerphone from yesterday evening.

She snatched up her phone and swiped the screen to answer. "Hello?"

A pause on the other end, and then a strange male voice said, "My name is Detective Inspector Ryan Chase. May I ask who I'm speaking to?"

Her mouth opened and shut. She was unsure how to respond. A detective? Why was a detective calling her? Immediately, she thought the worst. He was most likely calling because something terrible had happened to Russ.

"What's happened? Where's my husband?"

"I'm sorry, but I don't know that. Please can you give me your name?"

"Michelle. I'm Russell Mabry's wife. He's been missing since yesterday. Do you know what's happened to him?"

"I'm afraid I don't know that. This phone was found in relation to a crime I'm investigating. I'd like to come and speak to you about this in more detail."

A crime? Did that mean this detective thought Russ had been involved in something illegal? Russell never did anything illegal. In the ten years that she'd known him, she couldn't remember him even getting a speeding ticket. He was careful about everything, making sure every bill was paid on time and that they never went into debt. He was the most risk-adverse person she'd ever met.

"This...this can't be right. There must be some kind of mistake. There's no way Russell would ever be involved in a crime."

"You said your husband's name is Russell Mabry?"

"Yes, that's right." Hope bloomed inside her. They'd got the wrong man. She'd been right, and this was a huge mistake.

"Mrs Mabry, are you available to have a chat? I don't think this is a conversation we should have over the phone."

"Oh, yes, of course. I mean, I called the police earlier to try to get someone out to see me, but I was told everyone was too busy."

"We're not busy now. Are you at your home address? I'll be with you as soon as possible."

She went to reel off her home address, but he stopped her. "That's okay, we have your address."

"Right, yes, of course you do. I'll see you soon then."

The detective at the end of the phone said goodbye and ended the call.

She stood in the same position, staring down at the phone in one hand, the knuckles of her other hand pressed to her lips. She'd thought that the detective would give her answers, but instead she'd only been left with more questions.

A crime? Could her husband really have been involved in a crime?

Russell was the man who kissed her goodnight, who swung his son up into the air every time he came home from work. Yes, he was away at work most of the week, but she never for a moment thought she couldn't trust him. He'd never given her any reason to suspect he was doing something he shouldn't be.

Until the evening he'd never come home.

Chapter Thirteen

They pulled up outside a semi-detached house with what would have been a front garden turned into a drive with a drop curb. The curtain at the front window twitched, and Erica caught a glimpse of a woman's pale face through the glass.

"We've been seen," she said to Ryan.

He cocked an eyebrow at her. "Not like we're trying to hide that we're here."

"True. What do you think we're going to go into? Who is Russell Mabry, and what's his connection to Douglas Lloyd? Is it possible they're the same person? It wouldn't be the first time a man has kept two different families running, and the neighbours said Douglas Lloyd was away working a lot."

"It's certainly possible. Both names are clean when I've run checks on them, and neither has any kind of social media presence. The couple of photographs I've managed to pull up are from a distance or in group photos, and they're both men of a similar age with brown hair. I could get an analyst to try to make them clearer, but we don't have time for that right now. The wife is bound to have a photograph. We can compare it to ones we took from the first house."

Erica glanced over at the house. "They live a bit close together for that setup. He'd have been taking one hell of a risk not to bump into the other wife and child in the supermarket or cinema or something."

Ryan cocked an eyebrow. "Maybe they did find out about each other. Perhaps that had been the reason his family had been killed or he'd killed his family—the stress of trying to keep two lives going had been too much for him."

"You think he might have snapped?"

"It's a possibility." Ryan gave a low whistle and shook his head. "Takes some balls, though, doesn't it? I couldn't imagine living like that. He must have been on high alert every time he left the house."

Erica shrugged. "Or he was just one of those smug bastards who didn't give a shit."

"Or maybe the two families even knew about each other. That does happen."

"True. Plenty of women turn a blind eye to their husband's affairs, and it most likely happens the other way around, too."

"We don't mention any of that to the wife, though," Ryan said. "No point in putting ideas into her head."

Erica nodded her agreement.

They both climbed out of the car and approached the front door. It swung open before they'd even made it onto the driveway.

"Come in, please." Michelle Mabry beckoned them towards the house, her eyes wide. "But keep your voices down. My son, Max, is upstairs. He's got his headphones on and is playing games, but I don't want him overhearing our conversation."

Ryan had led the way, and she stepped back to let him through, Erica following close behind.

"This way," Michelle said, showing them into a tidy living room that looked as though it had been decorated in the style

TWICE THE LIE

of a magazine, not an item out of place, the pictures on the walls all coordinated, a thick cream rug on wooden floorboards. It was pretty but generic. "Please, sit down."

Erica perched on one armchair, while Ryan selected the two-seater sofa opposite. Michelle sat on the biggest of the seating on offer, but she leaned forwards, her hands clasped between her knees, her face drawn with worry.

"Mrs Mabry," Ryan started, "does the name Douglas Lloyd mean anything to you?"

She frowned and shook her head. "No, should it?"

"What about Elizabeth Lloyd, or Keira Lloyd?"

"No, I don't know them either. Please, my husband is missing. That's all I care about. I don't know who these other people are."

Ryan pulled out the photographs of the family that had been taken from their home and held them out to her. If this was her husband, she would surely react to seeing him with his arm around another woman and a young girl at his side. But Michelle's lips pursed, and lines appeared between her brows as she studied the picture.

"I'm sorry, but I really don't know who these people are. I've never seen them before. Are they connected to my husband's disappearance?"

Ryan exhaled a breath and sat back slightly. Erica studied his face for his thoughts. This wasn't going the way they'd anticipated. They'd suspected that Russell Mabry was an alias for Douglas Lloyd and that he'd been running two lives in secret from each other. But if the other wife didn't recognise the man in the picture, they were clearly wrong. Unless she was covering for him, of course, but this didn't seem like a woman who was covering for her cheating spouse.

"Honestly, Mrs Mabry," Erica said, "that's what we're trying to find out. We found a phone with your phone number on it hidden in this family's house."

"Why were you looking through their house?"

"The mother and daughter were tragically found murdered yesterday evening."

Michelle clapped her hand to her mouth. "Oh my God."

"The husband, Douglas Lloyd, is currently missing."

"Like Russell," she exclaimed.

"Yes, like your husband."

She burst into tears, put her face in her hands, her shoulders shaking.

Erica got up from the chair and sat beside Michelle on the sofa. "The thing is, Mrs Mabry, we really do need to find out how your husband knew Douglas Lloyd."

"He didn't hurt those people. I know he didn't. He couldn't have done such an awful thing."

"That's not what we're saying, but there's a possibility he might be in trouble, might even be hurt or in danger. The sooner we find him, the sooner we can help him." She didn't want to make any promises she couldn't keep, and she was aware that she was using Michelle's love for her husband and belief in his innocence for their own advantage, but it couldn't be helped. They needed to figure out what the hell was going on here.

"Can you think of anyone who might have wanted to hurt your husband?" Ryan asked.

"God, no! No one would. He's a good man, Detective."

"He hadn't mentioned falling out with anyone then, no matter how small it might have seemed at the time?"

"No, not at all."

Ryan clasped his hands between his knees. "Have you noticed anything odd about his behaviour recently? Strange phone calls, or anything like that?"

"No more than normal. He's always getting phone calls at stupid times, but it's part of his job. He deals with a lot of businesses that are on different time zones, and they just don't think about what time it is here when they call."

"And what is his job?" Erica asked.

"He's a pharmaceutical rep for NovoFord Pharmaceuticals."

Ryan took over again. "So, it's usual for him to receive phone calls during unsociable hours."

"Yes, but like I said, it's his work." Michelle looked between them both as though assessing what they thought of the situation. "Their head office is in America, and they have offices all over the world, which is why they call then."

He nodded. "Of course. That's perfectly understandable."

They didn't want this woman to get defensive and shut down on them. Right now, Michelle Mabry was the only real lead they had.

"Does your husband have an office in the house?" Ryan asked. "A place he works from?"

"Yes, he does." Michelle glanced towards the ceiling. "It's the box room, upstairs."

Ryan got to his feet. "Do you mind if we take a look?"

"Umm, no, I suppose not. It's this way."

Erica stood as well, and Michelle led them upstairs. She opened the door that appeared to lead onto a bedroom, then moved out of the way. Erica understood why the moment she'd stepped through with Ryan. The room was barely big enough to hold two of them, never mind three.

"I'm just going to check on Max," Michelle said. "Call out if you need anything."

Erica offered her a smile. "Thank you. We will."

The office was as tidy as the rest of the house. Ryan pulled on a pair of gloves, and Erica stood by the door while he opened drawers and flicked through paperwork. It wasn't that she didn't want to help, but the size of the space meant she'd be more of an impedance than an assistance if she tried.

"He has a company car." Ryan held up some paperwork. "Let's get a search put out on the license plate number."

Erica took out her phone and placed the call to control to get that actioned. When she was done, she turned her attention back to Ryan. "Anything else of interest?"

He shook his head. "Not that I can find. Appears to be the office of a normal married father of one, but there's something more going on here. I can feel it."

Erica dropped her voice so Michelle didn't overhear. "I don't think she has any belief that her husband has been doing something he shouldn't. She seems completely trusting of him."

"She wouldn't be the first wife to discover her husband is nothing like the person he's been making out to be all the years of their marriage."

Erica chewed her lower lip. "Could she be in danger? Her and the boy? It might be worth suggesting she goes and stays somewhere for a while."

He nodded in agreement.

"How are you getting on?" a female voice chirped out at them from the hallway.

Erica resisted the urge to jump guiltily. It wasn't as though they'd done anything wrong. She faced Michelle. "We're almost done. We've put a search out on your husband's company car, so hopefully that'll help track him down."

"Oh, right. I do hope so."

Erica continued. "Have you got a friend or family member you can stay with for a little while, at least until we can figure out what's happened to your husband."

Her eyes widened. "Why? What if Russ comes home and I'm not here?"

That's what we're worried about, Erica thought but didn't say. "We just think it would be safer if you were staying with someone else."

"Safer? You think I might be in danger? That Max might be in danger?"

She gave Michelle a kind smile. "We hope not, but it's just a precaution. Is there anyone you can stay with?"

"I can phone my mother. She'll be happy to have us, though she's going to want to know what's happened to Russ." Fresh tears trickled down her cheeks. "And what do I say to that? What *has* happened to Russ?"

"Right now, all we know for sure is that he's missing. That's all your mother needs to know, too."

Michelle sniffed and swiped at her cheeks. "Okay," she said quietly, and then more loudly, "Okay."

Chapter Fourteen

By the time they got back into the office, the forensic report had come in from the crash site.

Ryan read over it with interest, while chugging a cup of coffee and shoving a sandwich he'd picked up at the local corner shop down his throat. He'd washed his hands three times before eating, but somehow reading about blood spatters didn't affect his appetite.

There were two blood types found in the car, one of which matched with Douglas Lloyd's DNA. The second one was unknown. There was someone else in this picture, and he was starting to wonder if that other person could have been Russell Mabry. He would need to get a warrant for Mabry's house to see if they could match the DNA. More blood had been found nearby, and on the road. There had also been several different sets of fingerprints found inside the car and on the door handles.

Was Douglas Lloyd in the car willingly, or had he been injured and taken?

DC Lawson approached his desk. "Boss, I've been working on contacting each of the owners of the vehicles that we caught on the CCTV outside of the shop. I think I've found someone who saw something."

Ryan perked up. "Tell me."

"Fifty-two-year-old Alan Walsh was driving back from work. He passed the shop at five twenty-six and so he must have seen this literally moments after."

"Seen what, Detective?" Ryan said, getting frustrated.

"He saw someone stopped on the side of the road, just past our crash site. He said he swore under his breath at them because they were pulled over right on the narrow part and it wasn't exactly easy or safe to pass. There were three men around the car."

"That sounds like the people we're after. I want to speak to Mr Walsh myself. Have you got an address for him?"

"Sure do, boss. Here." She handed him a printout.

Ryan grabbed his jacket from the back of his chair and got to his feet. No time like the present.

TWENTY MINUTES LATER, he was at Alan Walsh's home, sitting on his sofa after having turned down the offer of a cup of tea from Mrs Walsh. Mr Walsh was a short, skinny man with a hooked nose and eyes set too deep in his face, but he seemed amiable enough and was trying to do everything he could to help.

"Thank you for talking with me," Ryan said. "Your information could be vital in us apprehending a very dangerous man. What time did you say you saw the car blocking the road?"

"It was about half past five. I drive by there at the same time every day on my way home from work."

"I don't suppose you managed to see what type of car it was?"

He wrinkled his nose. "It was red. A Honda, I think. An old one."

"What about the licence plate number?"

"Sorry. I didn't pay that much attention."

Ryan ignored the dip of disappointment in his gut. Even a fraction of the licence plate would have given them something more to go on, but the colour and make of the car would help.

"Can you give me a description of the people you saw?"

Walsh nodded. "They were all men. Two were middle-aged, a bit younger than me, I suppose. Maybe more your age. The other one was younger, in his twenties, I'd say. I think he was the one who was driving."

Ryan showed him a photograph of Douglas Lloyd. "Would you say this was one of the men you saw?"

He frowned and twisted his lips. "Could be, yes."

"What about this one?" He showed him a picture of Russell Mabry.

He shook his head. "Possibly, but it's really hard to say. I literally caught a glimpse, and I was more concerned about the fact they were stopped in such a dangerous spot than anything else. The two older ones got into the back seat, or at least it looked like one of them had to practically haul the other one in. I thought they were most likely drunk."

Ryan wished Walsh could have given a more definite ID since 'could be' was unlikely to get them a prosecution.

"Did they appear to be hurt at all?" Ryan asked.

Walsh twisted his hands together in his lap. "There was blood on one of the men's faces, and I think he was limping."

"But you didn't think to call for help?"

Alan Walsh shrugged and glanced away guiltily. "I assumed they had everything under control. I didn't know there was anything bad happening. I didn't really process what was happening until later. I was more annoyed that some idiots had stopped in the middle of a narrow road than anything else."

Ryan did his best not to let his frustration show. If only Mr Walsh had called in what he'd seen, they could have apprehended the suspects within an hour of Elizabeth and Keira Lloyd losing their lives.

"That's okay. The description of the car you've given us will be a great help."

Walsh leaned forwards, his face creased with concern. "I really hope you find whoever killed that woman and her little girl. It's hard to imagine what would drive someone to do such a terrible thing."

It certainly was, but people did terrible things every single day. That was why Ryan did the job he did—to make sure people like that ended up in the only place they deserved to be. Behind bars.

Chapter Fifteen

Erica's phone rang, and she answered the call.
"DS Swift."

"My name is PC Robertson. I'm phoning because we've located a vehicle that you've got an alert out on. A black 2018 Mercedes-Benz A-Class. It was located parked a couple of streets away from the double murder your team has been investigating."

She was already on her feet, gesturing at Ryan, who had only just walked back into the office after talking to a witness who'd spotted the car that might have picked up Lloyd.

"Don't touch it," she said to the officer on the phone. "We need to get SOCO onto it. It's potentially linked to that murder."

"Understood. I'll make sure no one goes near it until you get here.

"Thank you."

"We've found Russell Mabry's company car," she told Ryan before he could sit down. "It was only a couple of roads away from the Lloyd house."

He pressed his lips together, nostrils flared. "Damn. How did we miss it?"

"We didn't know we were looking for it until we linked Mabry to the murders."

"True. I don't suppose there's any sign of Mabry himself? Or Lloyd for that matter?"

She shook her head. "No, and he'd have to be an idiot to go back to it, but you never know."

"Come on, I'll drive," Ryan offered. "The engine's barely cooled yet anyway."

Within fifteen minutes, they reached the location of the car. Already, a crime scene tent had been erected to prevent the search from being watched by the gathering groups of pedestrians that were curious about the growing police presence. Houses lined both sides of the street, the upper floors giving everyone a good view down onto the car. The tent also helped protect what was now a crime scene from the weather, and there was rain threatening. Once they'd done their initial check of the car—in particular making sure there were no people, living or dead, inside it—they would load it onto a recovery vehicle, and it would be taken to a secure covered compound where a full forensic search would be carried out.

"Let's get it open," Ryan said, putting on a pair of protective gloves.

They broke into the vehicle. Erica was relieved there were no bodies hidden in the boot, or anywhere else. Neither was there any sign of the murder weapon. A couple of clear plastic boxes containing leaflets, branded pens, and other items clearly linked with Russell Mabry's job. It was the weapon they were after, however, something tangible to link him to the two murders and Douglas Lloyd's disappearance. Quickly, they went through the boxes, taking photographs of anything that might be relevant, then they took the boxes out of the boot and set them down.

Erica tore up the boot carpet to expose the items that replaced a spare tyre these days—a pump and a tyre repair kit. She lifted them out, and as she did so, a part of the side of the boot moved with it. She frowned. The plastic casing had been tampered with. It no longer covered the metal shell of the car but had been pulled away.

"Boss, look here."

Ryan moved to see over her shoulder.

She carefully worked out the piece of boot casing to reveal a plastic-wrapped block of white powder.

"Well, this just took a turn I didn't see coming," Ryan said.

"I'd take a good guess at it being cocaine."

He nodded. "That's most likely, but we're going to have to get narcotics in."

"Russell Mabry worked for a pharmaceuticals company, didn't he, and Douglas Lloyd sold medical equipment?"

"They're similar job roles," Ryan said. "Both would be driving around the country visiting hospitals."

Erica raised an eyebrow. "I don't think these are the kinds of drugs they're supposed to be selling."

"I'd say not, but I think we've finally got our motive."

She glanced over at him. "You think the mother and daughter were murdered because of drugs?"

"Seems that way to me. Maybe Douglas Lloyd did something to upset the people he worked for and this was their payback."

"And how is Russell Mabry involved?"

"Maybe he's the one Lloyd has been working for?"

Erica frowned. "Wait a minute, we only have drugs in Mabry's car, not Lloyd's. There's no proof that Lloyd has had any involvement with drugs."

"What about his company car?" Ryan double-checked. "Was anything found in there?"

"Nothing like this, but I'm not sure it was tested for narcotics."

"Looks like it's going to need to be tested again."

Chapter Sixteen

Phillipa Lowry had felt bad about sending Conner off to his dad's that morning, but not bad enough to keep him home. He'd done his best to make her feel sorry for him, saying how he'd had a late night after not getting back from the police station until almost eleven and then hadn't been able to sleep and had bad dreams all night. She hadn't bought it, though. Conner was tough, and she highly doubted a little blood and a crashed car had bothered him much. He'd probably enjoyed all the excitement. She loved her son, but he could be a bit of a handful. When she'd first broken up with Conner's dad, she'd thought she'd hate the weekends where Conner went and stayed with him, but over the years she'd come to look forward to having a bit of quiet time to catch up on everything. At least when Conner had been smaller, she'd had her evenings to herself, but now Conner basically went to bed at the same time she did. True, he did tend to hide away in his room, but it still wasn't the same as having the house to herself.

She walked around, picking up the numerous t-shirts and socks and boxer shorts from the floor.

"Jesus, Conner," she muttered to herself. "The basket is right outside your door. Is it really so hard to throw them a couple of feet?"

Why did she bother? It wasn't as though he could hear her.

She guessed she should be happy he was changing them, at least. At some point over the last few months, he'd gone from her having to nag him just to get in the shower, to him taking forever in there and wanting all the male skin and haircare products he could get his hands on.

Despite all the washing, the room still had that stale odour of teenage boy—even though he hadn't even hit that age yet—that no douse of air freshener or open windows seemed to shift. That didn't stop her opening the window, though. She glanced at the crumpled sheets on his bed and wrinkled her nose. They needed changing, too. If she got them in the wash now, she could have the same ones back on before he came home again tomorrow morning, and then he'd never know. He always complained when she came in his room, even if it was just to tidy up.

She pulled off the duvet cover and dropped it to the floor, then did the same to his pillow. Then she leaned across the single bed to yank out the corner of the fitted sheet. As she pushed her hand down the side, her fingers came into contact with the crinkle of empty crisp packets.

"Oh, for goodness sake, Conner!" she exclaimed, climbing half onto the bed to see down between the bed and the wall.

She was greeted by a medley of chocolate bar and crisp wrappers and empty cans of Coke. She loved her son, but he was a filthy little bugger at times.

There was no way she could leave all this mess, though she was tempted to. She grabbed his completely empty wastepaper basket off the floor and pulled a face as she scooped out handful after handful of rubbish and dumped it into the bin. She'd almost reached the floor when her fingers curled around something solid and cold. Curious, she drew it back up with her and glanced down at what lay in her hand.

Her stomach plummeted, feeling as though she'd been punched in the gut, her breath expelled from her lungs.

A knife—a kind of switch blade—the handle plastic, with metal nestled beneath.

It wasn't a small knife either. When she hit the button to open it, the blade was at least five or six inches. Dark brown smeared the blade and more spots on the handle.

Was that what she thought it was? Why did Conner have a knife covered in blood?

Her hand shook, and she dropped the blade onto the half-unmade bed. Her face burned while she felt as though all the blood had dropped to her feet. Her first instinct was to get on the phone to call his mobile and demand to know what he was doing with it, but then she hesitated.

What if Conner had done something terrible? What if he told her something awful that would change their lives forever?

No, she forced herself to think this through properly. He was eleven years old, and maybe he could get into a bit of mischief, but he wouldn't do anything as stupid as hurting someone else. He'd picked up the knife from somewhere, and after yesterday's events, she had a good idea where from.

Though she knew this to be true, it didn't loosen the knot in her stomach or stop her hands shaking. She needed to give Conner the opportunity to explain himself, and then she'd call the police. One of the detectives had given her a card the previous day, which Phillipa had put in her handbag. She could call the number on that. But first she would speak to her son.

Leaving the bloodied flick blade on the bed where she'd dropped it, she crawled back off the mattress and left the room in search of her mobile. She couldn't get her thoughts to straighten, and her mind was completely blank as to where she'd left it. In the kitchen? In her handbag? Beside her bed? She couldn't get the image of the blood on the blade out of her head.

Her gaze landed on her phone on her bedside table.

She snatched it up and swiped the screen to bring up Conner's number. What would she do if he didn't answer? She'd go crazy if she couldn't talk to him.

But he did answer. "Hi, Mum. We're in McDonald's. Dad bought me two burgers."

For once, she didn't care about what he was eating. "I found the knife down the side of your bed, Conner. Want to explain that to me?"

Her son fell silent.

"Conner?"

"It's not mine."

"Good. Then I suggest you tell me whose it is."

"It was on the passenger seat in the car we found yesterday. The car door wasn't shut properly, and I just slipped my hand through the gap and took it."

She sank to the edge of her bed. "Jesus Christ, Conner. What the hell were you thinking?"

"I don't know, Mum. It looked kinda cool. I wanted to have something to show everyone at school on Monday 'cause I thought they wouldn't believe me."

She wasn't even going to get into the fact her son thought it would be a good idea to take a knife into school. Sometimes it felt like he had no common sense whatsoever.

"You're going to have to tell the police," she said. "I'm phoning that detective now."

"No, Mum, please! I'll get in trouble."

"I really don't care if you're going to get in trouble, Conner. Maybe it'll make you think twice before you do something so utterly stupid next time."

"Mum, ple—"

But she cut him off. "Put your dad on the phone."

"Come on, Mum, please don't tell him."

Her voice was unusually hard. "Now, Conner!"

There was a rustle and a sighed breath as the phone was handed over. Phillipa always did her best to only speak to her ex when it was absolutely necessary, and it appeared now was one of those times.

"What is it, Phillipa?"

Harvey's cool tone wasn't going to affect her today.

"Your son came across a car accident yesterday that is linked to the murder of a mother and her little girl, and I think he stole what might be the murder weapon from the inside of the car."

"Fucking hell." His voice faded slightly. He must have turned his mouth from the phone to address Conner. "Is that true?"

She didn't hear Conner's reply, but it wasn't as though he could deny it.

"I'm calling the detective who's dealing with the case. I imagine they're going to want to talk to him, so I suggest you put the remains of your lunch in the bin, or bring it with you, and get him here right away."

"Yes, right. Okay. I'll bring him home now."

Phillipa ended the call, exhaled a long breath, and dragged her hand through her hair, then she got up and went to find her handbag to dig out the detective's business card.

Chapter Seventeen

Erica hung up the call and then went to track down Ryan at the coffee machine.

"We need to get down to Conner Lowry's house."

He took a sip from the plastic cup of still steaming coffee. "What's happened?"

"His mother has just called. She found a knife covered in what looks like dried blood hidden down the side of the boy's bed."

Ryan's blue eyes widened, and he dropped the full coffee cup into the bin nearby. "I had a feeling the boys had opened the car door. The SOCO report showed fingerprints on the door handle. I meant to talk to him myself."

"You'll get your chance now. The boy's mother says her ex-husband is bringing Conner home right away. He should be there around the same time we are."

"I don't want to think about what damage the kid's done to any evidence we might have got off the blade," Ryan said.

"Hopefully, there will be enough left that we can convict whoever killed that poor family."

They left the office and drove to the Lowry residence.

Erica climbed out, rounded the car, and opened the boot. She took out the evidence collection container—a plastic tube for the knife—and slammed the boot shut again. Ryan had climbed out as well, and he hit the key fob to lock the doors.

Erica approached the house, only to realise the DI wasn't with her. She turned back to discover him checking the car door to make sure it was locked, even though he'd already done it. She'd noticed him doing things like that a lot more often recently.

"Everything okay, boss?" she called out.

He faced her, his expression surprised, as though he hadn't quite realised what he was doing. "Absolutely."

He joined her on the doorstep, and she rang the bell. Phillipa Lowry answered the door, her eyes red and puffy from crying, twin streaks of mascara below them.

"Thank you for coming so quickly. I haven't been able to go up there since I found it."

"The knife you mean?" Erica asked.

"Yes, the knife that was used to kill that poor mother and daughter. Their blood is on it." Her voice shook as she spoke. "It's still on the bed where I dropped it. I couldn't bring myself to touch it again."

"You did the right thing, both by calling us and not touching it."

She dropped her gaze and nodded.

"Do you want to show us what room it's in?"

"Yes, of course."

She led them up the stairs. "Will...will my Conner be in trouble for this?"

"He's a minor. He'll get a warning, but that's all. Hopefully it'll be a lesson to him, and he'll think twice before doing something like this again."

"He's going to be grounded until he's eighteen, so I'm hoping the opportunity won't arise."

Erica exchanged a glance with Ryan. In both their experience, boys who liked to cause trouble continued to cause trouble, at least until they were grown men with responsibilities of their own, and even then, it was questionable.

Phillipa showed them to her son's room where the bed had been half-stripped, and the bloodied knife lay on the bed.

Ryan took a couple of photographs. "Was the knife open when you found it?"

"No, it wasn't. It was shut. I don't know why I did it, but I pushed the button to open the blade. That was wrong, wasn't it? I shouldn't have done that?" She shook her head and covered her face with her hands.

"It's fine," Erica reassured her. "We just need to get all the details. Do we have your permission to search the rest of the room as well? We'll bring in a crime scene officer to do it."

"You won't find anything else," she replied, a hint of panic to her voice.

"Probably not, but we still need to check."

Phillipa wrung her hands together. "I mean, if that's what you need to do, then yes, you have my permission."

"Thank you."

The click of the front door opening came from downstairs.

"That'll be Conner," Phillipa said.

"Good." Erica offered her a smile. "It's important that we speak to him."

"I'll talk to him," Ryan said. "Bag that up."

Erica nodded and proceeded to put on a pair of gloves to place the blade into the evidence collection container. The mother and son had probably done a lot of damage to any fingerprints they might have been able to get off the handle, but it was still possible the forensic scientists would find something of use. Even a partial fingerprint might be enough to convict someone.

As she placed it inside the plastic tube, she noticed a small sticker for a fishery stuck to the handle. Was it a fishing knife? She made a note to put it in the report, then took the knife back out to the car where she waited for her boss.

"What did he say?" she asked Ryan when he came out.

"Only that he noticed the knife lying on the passenger seat when he looked through the window. He said his friend didn't see him when he stuck his hand in the gap and picked it up and stuck it down the waistband of his jeans. When he leaned on the window again to make it look as though he'd been peering through the whole time, the door fully shut."

"Do you believe him?"

"Yes, I think so. I just wish he'd been truthful with us before. We could have made some headway on this case a lot sooner. I've put a call in to have the room thoroughly searched as well."

Ryan's phone rang, and he glanced down at it. "It's DC Lawson."

He answered. "Yes, Lawson, what have you got?"

He listened for a moment and his gaze lifted to Erica. "Hang on a second, I've got Swift here with me. Let me just put you on speaker."

He did as he'd said, and DC Lawson's voice came through the phone.

"I think we've tracked down the car that picked up Lloyd and Mabry. It was caught on CCTV a mile down the road, and we were able to blow up the image enough that we could make out the first part of the license plate number and match it to the description we were given. The car's registered keeper is twenty-four-year-old Alec McKenzie. Looks like the address we have for him is up to date. He has a couple of priors, minor offences, mainly. Public intoxication, unlawful possession of suspected stolen property, minor assault."

"He sounds like a delight," Erica commented.

"Guess we'll find out," Ryan said. "As soon as SOCO get here, we'll go and pay Mr McKenzie a visit."

ALEC MCKENZIE LIVED in a run-down flat not far from Bristol city centre. An old sofa had been dumped in what barely passed as a front garden, black bin bags of rubbish piled on top of it.

Erica nodded at the banged-up red Honda Civic parked on the street. "That's our vehicle. We'd better call for backup."

"We'll get it towed so we can do a thorough search," Ryan said. "If it's the right one, forensics will find blood inside."

"What's the bet Mr McKenzie won't be happy about losing his car?"

Ryan grinned. "Do we care? Let's go and see what he has to say for himself."

They approached the door, and Ryan knocked with a short, sharp rap. Music was coming from the property, and he knocked again, the sound authoritative.

Footsteps approached, and the door swung open. A young man with curly hair that was in need of a cut opened it and frowned at the two detectives standing on his doorstep. "Yeah?"

"Alec McKenzie?" Ryan asked.

"Who's asking?"

Ryan flashed him his ID. "Do you own a car at all, Mr McKenzie?"

"Yeah, I do. Why?"

"Would you mind pointing out to me which one is yours?"

His gaze shifted between them and then over their shoulders to the car. "Yeah, it's the Honda Civic parked over there."

"We'd like to come in and speak to you, if that's all right."

His eyes narrowed suspiciously. "What about?"

Ryan jerked his head towards the inside of the house. "I suggest we don't have this conversation on the doorstep."

"Fine." He backed away, letting them through. "It's a bit of a mess," he said as he followed them into the lounge.

He rushed around, plucking clothes off the furniture so they were able to sit down. He was left holding a bundle of dirty laundry in his arms which he dropped into the corner of the room.

"We're not interested in your housekeeping skills, Mr McKenzie," Erica said with a tight smile, having to raise her voice over the noise.

Then he remembered the music and crossed over to a small wireless speaker and switched it off, plunging the room into silence.

"No, of course not." He dropped to perch on the edge of a chair. "What do you need to speak to me about?"

"We have reason to believe you picked up two people involved in a double murder on Friday afternoon," Ryan said.

The blood drained from his face. "Oh, shit. You're talking about those two blokes the other day, aren't you?"

"You admit you picked them up?" Erica asked.

"Yeah, I stopped for them. I thought they needed help. I didn't do anything wrong, though."

Ryan's lips thinned. "I'm afraid we're going to need to ask you to come down to the station with us for a formal interview. You're not in any trouble, but it's important we track down these two men, and we're going to need your statement as a witness on record."

McKenzie's gaze darted between them. "Do I have any choice?"

"Only if you prefer to be arrested first."

Alec McKenzie let out a sigh. "Fine. I'll get my coat."

"COMMENCING INTERVIEW with Mr Alec McKenzie in interview room one. DI Chase and DS Swift are both present," Ryan said out loud for the sake of the recording. He went on to ask McKenzie's current address, date of birth, and current employment.

"Mr McKenzie, can you please tell me the make of the car you own and the registration number?"

McKenzie reeled it off.

"Thank you. Now, tell me what happened on Friday afternoon," Ryan said.

"Umm, well, I was on my way home, and I saw these two people by the road. One was hunched over, and the other one was holding him up. I could see they needed help right away, so I pulled over. I mean, it wouldn't make me a very good person to ignore them, right?"

"I'm sure you're a model citizen," Erica said, doing her best not to let the sarcasm lace her tone. She'd already seen his priors.

"So, I helped them in the car and said that I should take them to the hospital, but the man who wasn't so badly beaten up said he didn't want to go to there."

"What about the other man, the one who was worse off?"

Alec shook his head. "He was barely conscious. I don't think he had any idea where he was."

"But you didn't think to call nine-nine-nine?"

"No, the other man said not to."

Erica stepped in. "And you didn't think to question why he didn't want you to call the police or take them to the hospital?"

Alec shrugged. "It wasn't any of my business."

Erica exhaled through her nostrils, trying to control her temper. If he'd just called the police, they could have picked up both men within a couple of hours of the murder.

But Ryan had clocked something else. "Are you sure there wasn't something else that prevented you from calling us, Mr McKenzie? I see you have several priors. Did you actually not call us because you were trying to hide something from us?"

"Nah, you're jumping to conclusions. It's nothing like that. I'll admit that I don't exactly have a good relationship with your lot, and maybe that's why I didn't call, but it was more that I know how to mind my own business, and I didn't want to get caught up in whatever mess those two had got themselves into."

"But you still stopped for them," Erica said. "Why do that if you didn't want to get involved?"

"I didn't see how badly hurt the other one was until after I'd stopped. I thought they were just pissed or something."

"You didn't notice any blood on them?" Ryan asked.

"Well, yeah, but again, who hasn't had a big night and walked into something."

Erica cocked an eyebrow. "A big night? It was just past five in the afternoon."

"Friday afternoon," McKenzie pointed out. "Maybe they'd got off work early and had a heavy night."

Ryan laced his fingers together. "Are you working at the moment?"

"Not right now. I'm on benefits."

"Where were you before you picked up the two men?" he asked.

His cheeks flushed, and his gaze skuttled away. "Uhh, nowhere really. Just driving around."

Ryan didn't appear to be buying a word. "Mr McKenzie, you do understand that the reason we know someone picked those two men up, and then were able to track your identification and your address here, is because we have eyes everywhere."

"You didn't manage to track those two men down," he muttered. He clasped his hands between his knees.

He had a point, but Erica wasn't going to tell him that.

"We can find out where you were, Mr McKenzie," Ryan insisted, "so you might as well tell us."

He blew out his cheeks. "Fine. I was with some mates at The Rose Arms."

"You were at the pub?" Ryan confirmed.

"Yeah, but I wasn't drinking, I swear."

Erica and Ryan exchanged a glance. Erica thought they'd both put their money on the fact Alec McKenzie had drunk a few pints at the pub that Friday afternoon. It would explain why he'd let his guard down and picked up Lloyd and Mabry, thinking they were two new drinking buddies or something, and he hadn't wanted to call the police when he'd realised they were actually hurt. It had nothing to do with his dislike of the police and everything to do with him not wanting a drink-driving charge.

"As you know," Ryan continued, "there's nothing we can do to prove that now, so how about we focus on those two men. What happened after they refused to go to the hospital?"

"It was only one of them that refused," he said. "The other one didn't say much at all, and he was the one who really could have done with medical attention, though the one who was talking had a bashed-up face as well, like a broken nose or something, and I think his leg might have been injured, too."

"They were in a car accident shortly before you picked them up," Erica said.

He nodded. "Yeah, that makes sense."

"What happened then?"

"The one with the nose started getting angry, 'cause I really was insisting they get medical attention, you know? I'm not a complete arsehole. But the more I insisted, the angrier he got, so in the end I just stopped the car and let them out."

Ryan straightened. "Where did you drop them?"

"He got me to let them out near Purdown. I've no idea why, though. There's nothing there."

"Maybe someone else was coming to collect them? Did you see any other cars?"

"No, I don't think so."

"Purdown?" Erica asked. "What's out there?"

Erica pulled up the map on her phone. There was nothing out that way except fields and a fishing pond that the public could pay to fish at. That stopped her. She remembered seeing the sticker stuck to the handle of the knife.

Erica looked to her boss. "I think I know where he's hiding out."

Chapter Eighteen

Douglas Lloyd tried to groan, but he wasn't sure he was even making a noise in real life or if it was all in his head. When he willed his arms or legs to move, they also refused to comply, and he was so cold he felt like the chill was coming right from the core of him.

Where was he? If he could only get his eyes to open, maybe he could figure it out.

He remembered, though, oh, yes, he remembered. He didn't want to. Each time he thought of what happened, he died a little more inside.

His wife and daughter were dead.

That son of a bitch, Russell Mabry, had killed them, and then he'd taken him from his house. He'd tried to fight back and had attacked Russell while he'd been behind the wheel of Douglas's car, but had only succeeded in driving them both off the road.

That fucker had murdered his wife and daughter. Russell had been in their house, searching for the thing Doug had stolen from him, when Beth and Keira had come home.

The sales job was just a cover. Between them, they moved large quantities of cocaine around the country. Everyone thought drugs were taken by the lower class—the homeless and the benefit claimants and the students—but that wasn't the truth. There was a different class of drug-takers–the businessmen and women, the celebrities, the rich. They didn't want to be dealing with some dodgy person they'd found down the pub. They liked to buy their expensive cocaine from someone with good teeth in a suit who didn't cause any awkward questions when they were seen showing up at their million-pound houses and city apartments. They wanted someone respectable, at least on the outside.

He'd worked well with Russel up until recently. The two of them had met at a conference several years ago. They'd got chatting over some drinks, then shared a couple of lines in a toilet during the evening drinks party. He'd noticed how Russell always seemed to have the best of everything—suits and watches and expensive shoes, more than what their job could have afforded. And he was in the same position, a young family at home, both with wives taking care of a child. How could he afford all of that when he was supporting a young family? There weren't many families who could survive on one wage these days, even if that wage was a decent one.

It had taken a couple of cocaine- and alcohol-fuelled meetups when they'd been on the road for Doug to eventually build up the courage to ask Russell. Russell had responded by taking Doug out to his company car, lifting the lining of the boot, and revealing a large block of clingfilm-wrapped white powder. Then he'd asked him if he wanted in. It was easy. They sold in bulk to wealthy people, depending on where they were in the country. Think of it like Uber, only with drugs. Whoever was closest to the order was the one who filled it.

Russell was the one with the contacts. He did the big pickups and then divided it off to Doug. Doug handed over any money he'd made, minus his cut, to Russ. It had been running this way for years, until recently. Doug noticed how his orders were growing sparser, how he wasn't getting as big deliveries as he had before. When he tried to bring it up with Russell, he'd got blown off, Russ telling him that things were just quiet right now, it was only a blip.

Doug hadn't believed him.

He'd taken it upon himself to do some digging. Russell often took secretive phone calls, and when Russ had been distracted during one of those meetings, only two days ago, Douglas had slipped the phone into his pocket. He'd monitor it for calls and see if business really had died off. Maybe he'd even intercept a call from whoever was higher up the line, the person Russell dealt with, and ask a few questions for himself. He'd spent too long with Russell as his intermediatory, it was about time he spoke directly with the main man.

He'd never thought Russell had it in him to hurt his family. He swore he wouldn't have got involved if he had. But Russell must have realised he'd taken the phone and had come looking for it. He didn't know what had happened when Beth and Keira came home, but he assumed Beth had confronted Russell, and things had quickly turned ugly.

Now his family had paid the ultimate price, and Doug had the feeling he was soon going to join them. He didn't care anymore. He was happy to say goodbye to all the material things he'd thought were so important—things he'd put his family's life in danger for—and slip into the darkness that beckoned.

Chapter Nineteen

Ryan knocked on his boss's door, waited for her to call to enter, and then stepped into the room.

DCI Mandy Hirst was sitting at her desk, and she looked up as he walked in. "What can I do for you, Chase?"

"There's been some significant progress in the Lloyd double murder. I believe we now know where Russell Mabry was dropped off with Douglas Lloyd, and I have an idea about where they might be hiding out. I'd like to request additional backup in the form of extra officers and a dog unit, the helicopter, too, if that's possible."

She nodded. "Whatever you need if it means bringing them to justice. Have you got any idea what the full story is behind the murders yet?"

"We found a significant amount of cocaine in Mabry's company car and traces of the drug in Lloyds' company vehicle, too. We can't say for sure just yet, but it looks as though they've been using their job roles as pharmaceutical sales reps to travel around the country, dealing cocaine while they're there. From the way the house had been rifled through before the killing, my guess is Lloyd took something from Mabry, and when he was disturbed by the family, he killed them."

She pursed her lips and shook her head. "Jesus Christ, those poor people. You can have whatever it takes to apprehend the bastard responsible."

"Thank you, ma'am."

"Good work on finding them."

"We haven't found them yet, ma'am, and it was a team effort. Everyone has really pulled together on this."

"That's good to hear. Teamwork is everything in this job."

He agreed one hundred percent. Sometimes it was hard to let go of the need to do everything himself, wanting to make sure everything was done exactly right, so it was important to have people like Swift, and Mallory, and Penn on his team who he could trust.

"Do you think there's a possibility either of the men are armed?" DCI Hirst asked him. "Do you need an armed response unit as well?"

"I don't believe so, ma'am. The weapon used was a knife, and we have that in our possession now. We don't have any intel to say they have access to guns. I also have good reason to think both men are hurt—Lloyd possibly fatally. I think we should consider Mabry unarmed but dangerous."

"Very well. Whatever you think."

Not wanting to waste any more time, aware that he needed to get people mobilised before they lost light again, he proceeded to put everything in place that was needed to bring in Mabry and Lloyd.

WITHIN THE HOUR, HE had the teams ready to go at the location on the road where Alec McKenzie said he had dropped off Mabry and Lloyd. Checking satellite images of the area, he'd ascertained it was mostly lakes and fields, but there was a row of huts used for birdwatching.

His team stood waiting for his command—Swift, Mallory, Penn, plus several uniformed officers and the dog handlers. The helicopter was in the air, and Ryan would bring it in if either man tried to run, not that he thought Lloyd would be in any condition to run. He hadn't wanted to have it overhead yet, for fear of alerting them to the police presence. He also had an ambulance nearby since it was expected that they'd find at least one, if not both, men injured.

He raised his voice to address his team. "We have reason to believe Russell Mabry has knowledge of the fishery and knows this area, which is why he asked the driver who picked them up to drop them off here. Consider both Russell Mabry and Douglas Lloyd unarmed but dangerous."

There was a chance Mabry had moved on, leaving Douglas Lloyd for dead and making his escape. But if he was covered in blood and injured as well, with no way of contacting anyone, hopefully he'd decided he'd be better off laying low until the heat died down.

The fishery covered almost ten acres, but much of that was water. If either of them had tried to cross the water to cover their trail, it would make it harder for the dogs to track, though not impossible. Dogs could smell a track that was even a couple of inches under water.

Ryan went to the dog handlers. "We've been told this is the location the two men were dropped off. We have items of clothing from both of them–a t-shirt taken from the Lloyd house, and a jacket found in Mabry's car. We have reason to believe they were together initially, though there's a chance Mabry has dumped Lloyd, alive or dead, and made out by himself. Both men are injured, Lloyd more severely than Mabry as far as we're aware."

One of the dog handlers nodded. "Don't worry, the dogs will distinguish between the two scents. If they separated, we'll still find them."

"That's what I want to hear."

Swift joined his side. "Teams are ready to go, boss."

"Thanks, Swift."

They'd follow the dogs, but they also had uniformed officers sweeping the area for any clues. The handful of fishermen who would normally be sitting around the lake had subtly been asked to leave and questioned as to whether they'd seen anything suspicious. None of them had.

A bark came from the dogs.

"We've got a scent," one of the handlers called over his shoulder.

Ryan glanced at Swift. "Hope you're feeling fit."

She threw him a smile. "Not in the slightest."

"Me neither."

The dogs followed the road for several meters and then ducked through a gate to enter fields. The fishery was still some distance away, but the lake was visible, the water shimmering in the late afternoon sun.

He hoped Mabry and Lloyd were out there somewhere.

Chapter Twenty

It felt as though they'd already been going for miles, but when Erica glanced behind her again, the road was still in sight. They were moving at a brisk pace, and her lungs burned, her thighs ached, and the muscles in her calves twitched, threatening to cramp.

The dogs could have run far faster but were held back by the speed of the handlers. Erica was thankful for that.

The two DCs were with the uniformed officers, sweeping the area for any signs of the two men. She envied them their slower pace.

"Swift, look," her boss said from beside her, also out of breath.

He jerked his chin in the direction they were heading. Sure enough, the wooden structures of the bird-watching cabins were ahead of them, still a far enough distance to appear only as brown dots on the green landscape.

They kept going, the dogs barking.

Movement darted out from one of the huts.

A man. He glanced over his shoulder and set off at a lurching run. His arms swung as he tried to compensate for what appeared to be an injured leg that he was dragging along behind him. That must have been why he hadn't made a run for it before now. Perhaps he'd been hoping it would start to feel better before he tried to make a move.

"Is that Mabry?" Erica asked. They were too far away to get a proper identification on the man.

"I don't know," Ryan said, his brow drawn down in frustration. "We can't release the dogs unless we know for sure."

"Stop! Police!" Erica shouted, though either the man was too far away to hear her, or he ignored her on purpose and kept going.

Whoever the man was, he wouldn't get away. There were too many police around, and he'd never outrun the dogs, especially not injured. But there was still a fair distance between them, and he turned the corner of a different hut and vanished out of view.

"Fuck," Ryan swore.

"He can't get far," Erica said.

They approached the huts, the dogs getting there first. The animals stopped at the second hut, their barking and frenzied activity rising to a crescendo.

There wasn't any door to the wooden shelter, just four walls and a gap where a door should be, and a glass window that covered most of the far wall. Sitting slumped against the wall, his eyes shut, shirt drenched in almost-dry blood, was Douglas Lloyd.

"Get the paramedics," Ryan shouted to the uniformed officers nearby, before ducking into the shelter.

Erica kept going. "I'll go after Mabry," she called back to him. Then to DC Penn, who was nearby, "I need backup."

She rounded the last of the huts, and something hit her across the chest, sending her reeling back and gasping in shock.

He'd hit her with a two-by-four he must have found on the ground. Son of a bitch. An arm wrapped around her neck, choking her, hauling her back against the side of the cabin. She was already winded from slamming into the wood, and now her opportunity to draw in a new breath had been cut off. Her lungs burned, her chest tight. Even though she knew her fellow police officers were right around the corner, the bright flare of panic filled her mind that this was going to go horribly wrong. What if he killed her and she never got to see her family again?

But then she remembered Russell Mabry had been injured in the car accident and how he'd been half dragging one leg as he'd tried to run, and she lifted her booted foot and swung it backwards. Her heel connected with the leg he'd been dragging, and he howled in pain. The hold on her throat immediately released, and she sucked in a long breath and spun to face him. He was about to rush her when Ryan rounded the corner behind Mabry. Ryan collided with him, forcing Mabry to his knees, eliciting another yowl of pain from the wanted man.

"It's over, Russell." Ryan clipped cuffs around his wrists. "Russell Mabry, you're under arrest for the murders of Elizabeth and Keira Lloyd, and the attempted murder and abduction of Douglas Lloyd. You are also under arrest for the intent to supply class-A drugs. You do not have to say anything, but it may harm your defence if you do not mention something you later rely on in court. Anything you do say may be given in evidence."

"No, please," Mabry begged. "This has all just got out of hand. I didn't mean to hurt them! That son of a bitch Lloyd stole my phone, and I was looking for it when they came back. Beth kept saying she was going to call the police. I couldn't let her do that. My whole business has worked because I'd kept my nose clean, and if this was reported, I'd go to jail. There were drugs in the back of my car. A lot of drugs. I'd go down for it, and the men I work for have people in jail who would want to make sure I kept my mouth shut. For good."

"So, you stabbed her?" Erica said in disbelief.

"I didn't mean to! I threatened her with the knife. I thought it would be enough to stop her, but she said she wasn't going to let some arsehole with a knife tell her what to do. She'd almost dialled nine-nine-nine by this point. I couldn't let her dial that final nine."

"And what about the little girl, Keira?" Ryan growled. "Did you mean to kill her?"

"She wouldn't stop crying. I told her to be quiet, but she wouldn't. She was crouched over her mother making this awful noise. I tried to grab her to pull her away—I didn't know what I was going to do with her at that point, I just wanted her to stop—but she shook me off and ran for the stairs. She screamed, and I was sure the neighbours were going to hear. I put my hand over her mouth and nose, just to keep her quiet; that was all, I swear. But then when I took it off again, she wasn't moving."

Ryan yanked him to his feet. "I suggest you save all of this for your interview down at the station."

But Russell didn't seem to want to stop talking. "Doug came home. He rushed over to her, but then caught sight of Beth through the open doorway. He looked over at me, and I knew I didn't have any choice. I stabbed him in the stomach, but I couldn't kill him yet. I still didn't have the phone. But I also knew that I couldn't stay in the house in case someone had heard Keira scream and had called the police. I spotted Beth's car keys on the side and grabbed them. I'd parked a couple of roads away so that my car wasn't seen near the house, but it was too far to get Doug while he was bleeding. I just had to take my chances. I thought I'd managed to get away with it, but then that arsehole attacked me while I was driving and forced us off the road."

"You might as well save your breath," Ryan said. "You're going to be repeating all this all over again at the station in a formal interview."

A couple of uniformed officers joined them, and Ryan handed Russell Mabry over to be put in the back of a squad car and taken down to the station.

The paramedics had arrived and were working on Douglas Lloyd.

"You think Lloyd will live?" Erica asked him.

Ryan glanced back over towards the cabin. "Unsure yet. But considering both his wife and daughter are dead, and that he'll be going away for some time under drug charges, I'm not sure he'll even want to make it."

"Do we have enough evidence to charge Mabry with murder?"

"Absolutely. Russell Mabry will be going inside for a very long time."

Chapter Twenty-One

The paramedics insisted on checking Erica over, though she hadn't suffered anything more than a few bruises from Mabry's attack. Nevertheless, they wouldn't continue to let her work until they'd made sure nothing was broken, so she sat in the back of an ambulance and let them do what they needed.

It was late, but there was still a lot of work to do. The fishery was now a crime scene, Mabry would need to be officially interviewed, despite his confession when he'd been arrested, and they needed to tie in Lloyd's involvement with traces of drugs found in the boot casings of his company car.

She felt they owed it to Russell Mabry's wife to hear the news in person, rather than getting a phone call. Giving anyone bad news was never something she enjoyed, and she was about to tell Michelle Mabry that her entire life was about to be ripped out from under her feet.

Mrs Mabry had gone to her mother's house, at their advice, so, once the paramedics reluctantly let her go, Erica went to that address.

She rang the doorbell and stepped back.

The door swung open, and Michelle stood in the empty space, her eyes hollowed with shadows, her skin pale. Her lips looked chapped and sore from where she must have been picking and chewing at them because she'd been so anxious.

"Can I come in?" Erica asked. "I have some news."

"Yes, of course. Come through."

She led Erica into the lounge.

"We've located your husband, Mrs Mabry," Erica said.

Michelle's legs seemed to go out from under her, and she sank onto the sofa. "Oh, thank God. Is he all right? Is he alive?"

"Yes, he's alive. I'm afraid he's been charged with the double murder of a mother and daughter, the attempted murder and unlawful imprisonment of another man, and intent to supply class-A drugs."

She shook her head frantically. "What? No, that can't be right. You must have the wrong person."

"I'm sorry, but we don't. It's definitely your husband. We're going to need to ask you to come down to the station so we can ask you some questions."

"You've made a mistake. Russell is a good man. He's a good father." A tear trickled down her cheek. "What am I going to tell my son? How would we manage for money?"

Erica understood that it was easier to believe the police had it wrong than consider the possibility they were right.

"We'll make sure you have the support you need to figure out your next steps," Erica told her.

"I won't believe it," Michelle insisted. "My husband is innocent. You've made a massive mistake, and before long you'll be apologising to both of us!"

Considering the amount of evidence they had against him, that was highly unlikely. But it wasn't unusual for a wife to stick by her husband, no matter what facts were presented to them. Over time, Michelle would realise the man she married was nothing like what she'd thought, and she'd carve herself out a new kind of life, one where her husband and the father of her child was a murderer. Erica felt sorry for the boy as well, having to grow up with that stigma hanging over his head, but she felt even more sorry for little Kiera Lloyd, who would never get the chance at a life at all.

Her phone rang as she helped Michelle into the back of her car to be taken in for questioning.

It was DI Chase.

"How did it go?" he asked.

"Much as expected. What about Douglas Lloyd? Is he still with us?"

"They've stabilised him. It looks like he'll pull through."

"That's good, I guess."

She wasn't sure she'd want to regain consciousness knowing her family were dead and she was facing a long spell behind bars if she were Lloyd. She didn't have a whole lot of sympathy for him, though. His actions had brought about the murders of his wife and daughter, and they were the true innocents in all of this.

Ryan's voice brought her focus back round.

"Thanks for all your work on this, Swift," Ryan said. "You'll be after my job one day."

"Thanks, boss."

Erica hoped she had the makings to be a good detective inspector at some point in her future. But, for now, she would be content to go home to her baby girl and husband.

It had been a very long day.

DID YOU ENJOY 'TWICE the Lie'? DI Ryan Chase is getting his own series, with book one, 'Kill Chase', now available to order from Amazon!

And if you haven't come across Erica Swift before, she has a six book series already out. Start with 'The Eye Thief' – you won't regret it! All books are available to read for free with a Kindle Unlimited subscription.

About the Author

MK Farrar had penned more than ten novels of psychological noir and crime fiction. A British author, she lives in the countryside with her three children and a menagerie of rescue pets. When she's not writing—which isn't often—she balances out all the murder with baking and binge-watching shows on Netflix. You can find out more about M K and grab a free book via her website, https://mkfarrar.com

Also by the Author

DI Erica Swift Thriller series
The Eye Thief
The Silent One
The Artisan
The Child Catcher
The Body Dealer
The Mimic

Crime after Crime series, written with M A Comley
Also available in audio
Watching Over Me: Crime after Crime, Book One
Down to Sleep: Crime after Crime, Book Two
If I Should Die: Crime after Crime, Book Three

Standalone Psychological Thrillers
Some They Lie
On His Grave
In the Woods

Printed in Great Britain
by Amazon